*Ma*dison
Retro

A NOVEL BY LARRY W. PHILLIPS

Waubesa Press
P.O. Box 192
Oregon, WI 53575

First Edition
ISBN 1-878569-22-8

Published by Waubesa Press, Oregon, WI
Cover design by Thill Design of Middleton.
Printed by BookCrafters of Chelsea, MI

Sincere appreciation is due to Marv Balousek for his generous assistance, suggestions and comments.

Special thanks to Pete & Vicki

OTHER BOOKS BY LARRY W. PHILLIPS
Ernest Hemingway On Writing (Charles Scribner's Sons)
F. Scott Fitzgerald On Writing (Charles Scribner's Sons)

*F*or David Zucker, Jim Abrahams and
        Jerry Zucker
            ...For contributions from a Long Ago Time

...And Doug & Lucy, Steve, Herm, Tim, Don, Pam, Lynnette,
Wart & Jan, Aleta, Wynn, Ralph, George, Rhonda, Judie,
        Berg & Sue...
            ...and others who were there

1
1994

Art Perriwinkle's Time Machine was located in his basement. His mother opened the screen door to let us in and we flipped on the basement light and went down to it.

It was about what you'd imagine: a cross between one of these large-sized electronic video games you find in a shopping mall, and one of these snap, crackling and popping get-ups you sometimes see in such late-night movies as "The Bride of Frankenstein" — a conglomeration of bells, dials, cylinders and blinking lights. There was a plastic helmet affair on top with a tangle of wires leading to it, built around what looked like an old exercise bike, and some other equipment that was blinking and humming, and the whole area around it looked like IBM's downtown headquarters — banks of computer screens, digital read-outs, green luminescent displays of varying types. Frankly, I was impressed.

"Nice job, Art," I said.

We both looked at it together.

Art's face glowed. I smiled to myself a little — actually, it was about what I expected to see.

"You sit on that," I said, "and you pedal or what?"

"No, you don't pedal," Art said. "You just sit there."

"And it takes you back through time?"

"No," Art said. "What I'm telling you... it's *from* then — a few years ago — I designed it then. It brought me to, well, right now..."

"It brought you to now," I said.

"Yeah."

I frowned. "Art..." I said.

"What?"

"Well, what does that make me, Art?" I asked, "Am I just like scenery for your trip ahead in time? I've lived the last few years — that's how *I* got here—"

"I know you did," Art said.

I continued: "—I didn't take a boat, a train—" I looked at it again "—or an exercise bike. I'm not just an accessory to your situation here."

Art dismissed me with a wave of his hand, and laughed.

"But in a way you *are*," he said. "That's the beauty of it. The software of it, you might say, merges with your software."

I frowned again. Art was always a little different. We went way back, Art and I, to college and even farther back, all the way to high school and grade school. Which is, now that I think about it, probably why he chose me. He needed someone who'd always been around, in every era of his life.

But, Art — yeah. He was one of those nerdy guys in high school — the ones who go to chemistry class, or physics, or math, and in the first week they pick it up — *all* of it. It makes perfect sense to them. Their brains are configured that way. While the rest of us are exchanging glances, like, God, what are we doing here? Meanwhile they're already taking notes and penciling in the answers. And when we got to college it was the same — Art lived in the same dorm I did as a freshman. He was the kid in the dorm who hot-wired the elevator so it only stopped at our floor — that sort of thing. When you asked him

how long it took to do that, he'd say— "about two minutes."
You could always find him sitting in his room, surrounded by
books, piles of them. Always reading. And not just math and
physics books either, all kinds — philosophy, psychology... One
look at Art, and you thought: this guy is going somewhere. It
might not be anywhere glamorous, but he's going somewhere.
He'll be the guy who invents, like, a diode or something like
that. That was the feeling you got, meeting him. He was
always sitting in the corner of his room, I can picture him even
now — short, bushy-haired, wearing these metal-rimmed glasses,
riveted on some book. That was Art. I hadn't seen him much
in the last few years, but he had come back from wherever he
had been, and now he didn't live far away.

Anyway, now it's twenty-five years later and we're both
45 years old and he's trying to sell me on the idea of a Time
Machine. Of course, I didn't believe it for a moment, but what
are friends for? You call them up — they come over. If they
come up with some farfetched or screwy idea, you were obli-
gated to listen. Also, I did have a vague feeling that if anybody
could pull it off, it was probably Art.

"Be a lot easier to go backward in time—" I suggested
"—to something that's already happened, than forward to stuff
that hasn't happened yet, wouldn't it?"

Art threw his hands up in the air. "Are you kidding?
There's no comparison!" he fairly shouted. "The past, it's so..."
he searched for a word— "It's so *specific*. It already *happened*.
Its a piece of cake compared to trying to get to the future."

"A piece of cake," I repeated.

I walked over to the machine — looked at the lights,
monitors and digital read-outs — a collection of hi-tech stuff
half encased in a dark curved partition. It was sitting a few
inches off the ground on one of these wooden palettes that
you see guys in forklift trucks carrying around.

"So what's the deal," I said. "You sit on this seat here and then—?"

Art shook his head. He walked over and flipped a few switches, but nothing appeared to happen.

"It's a force field," he said. "You don't have to be sitting on it. You can be just, well—" he gestured around him, "near it here in the field."

"That's great, Art," I said. "Well, let's get it over with. When does it start? Why don't you turn it on?"

"I did. It is on."

"Oh, it's on," I said. "Well, how come I don't feel anything?"

Art smiled.

"You don't feel anything," he said cryptically. He smiled to himself.

"Yes, that's right, Art," I said. "I don't feel anything. Except I'm getting a little annoyed."

Above me, to the left, I saw a crack of light appear at the top of the stairs and heard a voice. It was Art's mother.

"Art, I'm making sandwiches for lunch. Are you hungry? Would your friend like something to eat?"

"Yeah, Ma," Art called up, "We'll be up in a minute."

"Okay," she said. The door closed and the crack of light from upstairs disappeared.

Art peered at me quizzically, intently, like he's waiting for something to happen. He brought his face up close to mine, peering at me, in the fashion of a scientist looking at a bug specimen.

"Tell me what you're feeling," he says, very interested-like.

"What am I feeling?" I said.

"Yeah, exactly."

"Well, not much, Art, to tell you the truth. Not a thing, really. Is this a joke or something?"

"No, go on, tell me — what are you feeling? Give me your innermost thoughts," he said.

"My innermost thoughts? Okay... I'm feeling a little

foolish, number one," I said. "I mean, if you want my inner-most thoughts — here we are, two 45-year-old guys standing in a basement... We're adults, Art, what the hell are we doing here? And look at this thing—" I pointed at the machine. "We're acting like two high school kids with a crystal radio set, and your mother is upstairs making us some sandwiches... and for all I know probably some milk and cookies too."

I thought this answer would deflate him, but no, he seemed delighted by it. It seemed to be exactly the answer he was looking for. The lenses from his eyeglasses flashed in the basement light. And I *was* starting to feel a little odd, too, even if I wasn't saying it.

We were standing in the basement that Art's folks had converted into a kind of den or *rec room*. There was a large rectangle of brown carpet, a couple of tattered old sofas set at right angles, and a black and white TV in the corner with an ancient rabbit ears on top. It reminded me of when we were kids — we came here a lot in the summertime. We'd go outside to play, I remembered, and then we'd come inside later and cool off. We had spent a lot of time here in the summer. There was always a wonderful, cool, earthy smell to it — a kind of underground root-cellar aroma. It smelled terrific. It was also about 30 degrees cooler there on a hot summer day.

"You know, we used to come here a lot as kids, didn't we Art?" I remarked, looking around.

Art smiled knowingly. "That's it," he said softly.

"What's it?" I said.

"That's the feeling."

"The feeling—"

"You remember you said we were like two high school kids looking at a crystal radio set?"

"Yeah."

"Well think, Nick," he said. "Think very hard... doesn't that seem... familiar? Doesn't that sound like something you said a long time ago, in the past... Like we were...?"

"I don't—?"

He pointed to a table in the corner. "What's that?" he

asked.

I shrugged. "A crystal radio set," I said matter-of-factly.

"Was it here when we came in?"

I looked at it. I couldn't remember. I was feeling a little disoriented suddenly, and mildly confused.

Art didn't say anything for a moment. Then he interrupted the silence.

"Let's go upstairs and get something to eat," he said. "I've got something else I want to show you." He walked over to the machine in the corner and pressed down on a couple of switches.

"You've got something else to show me?" I said. "What?"

"1969," he said with a glint in his eye, "Upstairs its 1969."

2

Upstairs, seated at a small formica table in the kitchen, Art and I ate lunch. Egg salad sandwiches and Red Dot potato chips and, I thought, it was true, his mother did look younger, somehow. There was something about it. I couldn't put my finger on what it was. But as I watched her bustle about the kitchen, wearing her long dress and white apron, something was different.

"Don't you think you ought to get a haircut, Art?" she remarked offhandedly, while Art ate his sandwich hungrily.

He winked at me.

"So what's the theory behind all this?" I said, when his mother had momentarily disappeared into the other room.

"All time exists at once," Art said, his mouth full. "Past, present and future. It also involves us too — we're a big part of the equation. Time really happens in a synapse in the brain — it's just a very short leap of fire, like a... spark-plug in a car." He took another bite of his sandwich and winked again. Then he added: "Time is also space, of course, which is another equation."

"I'm afraid I don't understand," I said.

Art smiled cheerfully, a patient look on his face.

"Any compression of events slows time down," he said. "Pain, drudgery, agony — all slow time down. It's like a series of electric doors, like those you see in supermarkets — say, twenty in a row — that you walk through. If things are going badly, each one slams in your face. The days slow to a crawl. But if everything is going happily and smoothly, it's like each door opens automatically just as you come to it, and time speeds up... In an odd way, it sets up a kind of negative reinforcement. What it's really saying is: become a little unhappier in the future or another twenty-five years will pass just as quickly as the last twenty-five did." Art paused to take a drink of milk. He continued: "Yeah, so it's *problems* that start the electric doors slamming in your face as you come to them — which slows time down. You simply have to develop more problems in your life, Nick, or you're going to turn into an old man very quickly."

He laughed suddenly, putting me on.

I shook my head. "What has all this got to do with—"

"Nothing," he said. "I was just thinking out loud. But it is a kind of compression, a crowding-together of events..."

"Uh-huh."

"As you get older, there are gaps in time. We grow comfortable with things, our minds get less focused, start to drift... You might even say that we start to live every other moment instead of every one. And this moves things along. We skip over various moments, and time accelerates..."

I didn't say anything.

"Time is much more efficient than consciousness," he went on. "Time zips along very efficiently, while consciousness lurches along from point to point, missing much. 'Where did all the time go?' people ask. This is where. They were half asleep a good part of the time. Of course, we tell ourselves that we are *always* conscious, steadily and alertly so, but somewhere deep inside us we suspect the truth... that we are missing a lot in between. Meanwhile time is zipping along on its business-like way..." Art laughed again and slid out his chair and got up and got something from the kitchen counter.

"Art, would you and your friend like some cookies?" his mother asked, coming back into the kitchen.

Art winked again. "Sure, Ma," he said.

"So you're telling me it's 1969—" I said to him after his mother had left again, "What — in this house, outside, everywhere?"

"Sure — everywhere. Go take a look."

I got up and went to the window.

"It doesn't look any different to me," I said.

"See any cars older than 1969?" he asked.

In the distance I could see a large, old-fashioned-looking green dump truck. On either side of it cars stood ranged in rows along the street, four or five of them. It was true, they were all mid-Sixties era. But it could have been a coincidence. I was struck by how large they looked sitting in the street.

"Okay, you got me on that one," I said. "Everyone on your street owns a mid-Sixties junker," I said.

Art was busily stuffing some cookies in his mouth.

"See any rust on 'em?" he asked.

I looked. "No," I said.

"Odd, isn't it? For a cold weather climate?"

I looked at him.

"Ask my mother what the date is," he said. "Go ahead." His mother had gone in the living room and was now sitting in a stuffed easy-chair.

"All right," I said. I went to the hallway that led into the living room. "Mrs. Perriwinkle, what's the date?" I asked.

"Why, it's March 29th, Nick," she answered.

"What year?" I said, trying to sound casual.

"What year?" she said, turning half toward me, giving me a curious look.

"Yeah."

"Why, 1969 of course."

"Of course it is," I said. "Thanks Mrs. Perriwinkle." She continued to look at me curiously.

"Okay, Art," I said, "You cued your mother in advance

to say it was 1969."

Art smiled.

He got up and walked over to the wall and took the black phone receiver off the hook and held it out to me. Then he pulled out the telephone book laying on the counter and held it out likewise.

"Call any number in the book," he said. "Pick one at random and ask them what the date is, and the year."

I took the phone book from his hands. I thumbed through it and picked a name at random and dialed the number. A woman's voice answered. I didn't realize until then how ridiculous it was going to sound.

"Excuse me," I said into the receiver, "I'm from out of town — could you tell me the date?"

"March 29th," the surprised voice said.

"What year?"

"What year?" the puzzled voice said.

"Yes, we're trying to settle a bet," I said. Good, I thought — that sounded good. "Could you just tell me what year it is?"

"What year is it?" the voice asked again.

"Yes, like, is it 1994, or is it 1969?" I said.

"It's 1969," the voice said.

I hung up the phone.

There was a tone of certainty to it. I was listening for that. If it was a trick, it was a dandy.

"Okay, Art," I said. "I don't know how you did it, but she said it was 1969, too."

Art's mother reappeared in the kitchen. In a kind of stage whisper she said: "Art, is your friend all right?" — meanwhile looking at me.

"Oh, he's fine, Ma," Art said.

3

"**O**kay," I said, "for the sake of argument, let's say it's true, and that it works — what are you going to use it for?" We were down in the basement again looking at it. Art had flipped some switches and the contraption had groaned to a stop in the fashion of a dying vacuum cleaner, and it was 1994 again.

I was still not convinced. Art was capable of sleight-of-hand as well as electronic wizardry. He was capable of illusions as well as technical achievements.

"I had a friend who died," he said suddenly, seriously, "—died of AIDS. I don't know — maybe it's a dumb idea, but I thought I'd go back and look for Patient Zero."

"Who is Patient Zero?" I asked.

"Patient Zero," Art said. "He was the first identifiable subject who had AIDS. The very first case. I did some research on him. I know he passed through Madison on a certain weekend in 1969."

We were holding this conversation in my (and Art's) hometown, a place called Monroe in southern Wisconsin near the Illinois border — a small farming community. Madison, the state capitol, was about fifty miles away to the north.

"I didn't know anyone had AIDS back then," I said.

"The very first cases," Art said. "It was just starting. Nobody knew about it."

"Okay," I said, "so you go back, you find this Patient Zero. Then what? What do you do?"

"I don't know," Art said. "I haven't planned that far ahead. I just know I have to find him."

"You just want to find him? And then what?"

"I don't know — maybe I'll know what to do when I see him. Maybe it'll come to me. I'm hoping..."

I looked at him, but said nothing. Great. Art wants to go back in time and find a guy with AIDS, then do something, he's not sure what.

Art was thinking, mulling it over.

"You know, you were always good with the women, Nick," he said finally, "That was the difference between you and me. I really only had one girlfriend — one. In my entire life. I'm 45 years old. I'm kind of introverted and..." He laughed and held his arms out. "Look at me," he said.

It was true. The only thing missing was a pocket protector and a calculator — or, in 1969, a slide rule.

There was a moment's pause. Finally, he said:

"Her name was Amy, Nick. She died in 1982 from AIDS. I've got to go back. I've got to do something, now that I've got the chance... I don't know what..." he trailed off.

"So why don't you just go back and find her," I suggested, "Forget this Patient Zero guy and go find her instead?"

Art hesitated. "The thing is, I only knew her a couple months," he said. "I'm lucky I didn't get the disease myself. I just met her, Nick. I've thought about this a lot. I've got to go to the source. It's the only way. She must have known this guy."

We both fell silent. Finally, I said:

"Art, could I ask you a couple of questions about this time-machine business?"

"Sure," he said. "Shoot."

"Something's been bothering me. I mean, if you've invented this now, then wouldn't it be quite commonplace, say, in the future?"

He shrugged, as if the question was of little importance.

"—And if it was commonplace," I continued, "then wouldn't we be getting visitors from say, the year 22,000 or something like that? I mean, wouldn't people of the far-off future be coming back to visit us? You see what I'm saying?"

Art paused a long time on that one.

Finally he answered:

"My only guess is that something must happen to me."

"Oh, great," I said. "In other words, you're saying that it doesn't get extended into the future."

"That's right," he nodded, "For some reason it doesn't get extended into the future."

"Well, that's enlightening," I said. "And you want me to go along with you on this?"

"Yeah," he said. "I need you, Nick. I need somebody like you to go with me. You function better among people than I do. I'm a researcher, Nick, a scientist."

I thought about it for a moment.

He added with a smile: "Besides, I need some company."

"Okay," I said. "Let's say I go along. Let's say I've thought it over and decided to go along. I've got a couple of research projects of my own that I could pursue — one is a girl named Ida. From back then. I wouldn't mind seeing her again."

"Yeah?"

"Yeah. Well it's tempting you know. I mean if all of this is true. If this whole thing isn't a gag."

"It's not a gag. It works."

A picture of Ida flashed through my mind. Sweet, sentimental thoughts accompanied the picture, the kind that usually accompany images of the past.

"Yeah, I wouldn't mind seeing Ida again," I said, thinking out loud.

Art smiled.

"And you're sure this thing works?" I asked.

"It works," Art said again. "I've tried it."

"We can split up once we get there," I said. "Can't we?"

"'Get there, I like that," Art said. "It's not like that. It's here, Nick. The past takes place here. Right here... all around us. It's not like geography — a place you go to."

"All right," I said.

We looked at each other for a moment and then there was a silence. Then I said:

"Anything I need for the trip?"

Art smiled to himself and shook his head.

"They've got everything you need there — the past is a capitalist country, remember? You can buy anything you want."

I took a deep breath. We walked up the basement stairs together. I still didn't believe a word of it. And then the thought occurred to me that maybe I was losing my mind. On the way out the door I thanked Mrs. Perriwinkle for the lunch. This time she looked like she was about 80 years old.

4

I held out my hands, palms upward, to show I was help-less — that it was out of my hands. "I'm a photogra-pher, Art," I said. "What can I say?"

We were having a beer at the bar in Doyle's Irish Pub, a local restaurant in downtown Monroe. Art had fallen silent, looking down at the floor, disappointed. He said nothing.

"Art," I said, "June is coming up. It's right around the corner. Do you know what that means? Have you ever heard the expression, *June brides*, Art? Or *June weddings?* I'm booked up, Art. If you're a photographer, in June you're booked up — that's the way it works. I don't think I can take off."

"I understand," he said.

I tried to explain further: "—These brides, they book these things about a year in advance. It's their big day. You can't just call them up two weeks before the wedding and say that you're sorry, but you can't make it. It doesn't work that way."

"Okay," Art said again, still looking downcast, "I under-stand." He was kind of overplaying it, I thought, looking at the floor and all. A little too theatrical.

Okay, I thought finally — hell... Like all photographers, I had a short list of other photographers I could call up, other people in the business, favors you can call in if you really have to — if some emergency came up that was grave and pressing — and you just couldn't do it. But even then you didn't like to call them because then you owed them, practically forever. Besides, it was just something you didn't like to do to somebody. It was like asking somebody if they would spend their Saturday afternoon changing the oil in your car — at least it was for me.

"Would you mind ruining your whole weekend to do this instead?" That was what you were asking. But okay, Art, I thought, I'll see what I can do.

In the end I made some phone calls and a rival photographer inherited three months worth of my weddings. Now I had to be nice to him practically forever. I owed him. I could also expect a call sometime in the future — when I least expected it, or needed it — to go out and shoot some weddings for him. That was the unwritten code of wedding photography.

"You asked the other day if there was anything you needed for the trip," Art said. "Well, there is one thing."

"What's that?"

"A list."

"What kind of list?"

He shrugged. "A list of things you want to do, or see."

"Yeah?"

"Yeah — places to visit, things you wished you'd have done, or want to see, or people... that sort of thing..."

I nodded. "Oh, I get it."

He said: "It's just a matter of thinking it through, that's all, since you have this chance... I mean, instead of just going back and randomly wandering around. At least, I've always found it helpful... So make a list of... things you want to see again, that sort of thing."

I went home and thought about it. It made sense. If you were going to do it, at least be systematic about it — have a plan. But when I tried to do it, it was surprising. It was harder than I thought. Most people would automatically jump at the chance, but for some reason it was difficult to answer the "why" part of it... The "why" seemed rather vague... What things did I wish to see? What people or events? And why? In a day or two I produced a list. It was probably the same list anyone would come up with after thinking about it. But some of it still seemed rather vague even after I had written it down. The list looked like this:

Reasons to go back:

(1) To look up old friends; to see them again — as they were then.

(2) To see if I felt different — to see if I was a different person back then. Also, to experience the certain feeling again, of the era — was it simply a feeling of youth? To possibly see what it was like to feel young again...

(3) To experience the historical reality one more time — to see a different age, a different way of thinking. To experience the mood of the time.

(4) To see Ida. To see her one more time. Definitely. Possibly to re-live certain aspects of one's life that now, years later, you might have done differently at the time.

(5) To see the reasons why certain things happened. For instance: Why exactly did Ida and I break up? I've always wondered about that. I could never quite remember. For years I had asked myself this, but the reason was hidden in the mists of time... What was the exact conversation that led to it?

(6) To see what happened at a certain moment in time that you have always wondered about ever since. Some conversation or sight or event that might have changed your life... Or, possibly, to see why your life moved in a certain direction — to see what influenced it at a certain time... Was it an article you read, a book, a chance remark?

(7) Lately: annoyed and disheartened with the modern era. Irritated with certain aspects of the modern age — crime, politics, the business world, faxes, computers, cellular phones... the whole lot of it. I wanted to see again a more idealistic age — if indeed it *was* more idealistic. I wanted to go back to simpler times... (*Were* they simpler? Or was it something I just imagined?)

(8) To find myself... in other words, who I was, originally. Sometimes you lose who you were — the real you — over time... Changes occur which are so gradual that it is hard

to really remember — or be sure — that you are the same person, or that you remember your former self accurately. Are you the same person you used to be, or did you gradually change into someone else?

(9) To take some photos. As a photographer I'd wished for years I'd taken more photos at the time.

(10) Possible option: to see certain rock bands of the era... Janis Joplin, Jimi Hendrix, the Doors, Led Zeppelin...? This one seemed like a long shot, but after hearing some of the songs over the radio for years since then, I wanted to see for myself.

There was one final reason. Call it Reason No. 11.

There was another girl — a second girl. Her name was Lakey. She was a petite blond who had worked briefly as a receptionist in my photography business. I'd only known her for a couple years, but she was a good friend. While she had been the most vibrant, beautiful woman you could imagine when I had first met her, her face now had a lined, weather-beaten look and she seemed despondent. Her father had died in early 1994 — of a heart attack, brought on by excessive drinking — and she had taken it hard. His death had taken a great physical toll on her. She no longer resembled the person I had originally known. Her father had lived in Madison at the time. I wanted to talk to him. Like Art, I didn't know what I had in mind, or what I wanted to do about this situation, but I wanted to try to do something.

The list still felt incomplete somehow, but I brought it with me to Art's house and showed it to him, and he read it thoughtfully. I thought it was a pretty weak effort, but he seemed to approve.

"So you want to find this girl... Ida?" Art said.

"Yeah."

He was silent for a moment.

"And... you want to look around?" he said, reading.

"Yeah, basically," I said. "I don't know... I'd just like to see as much as possible."

Art fell silent for another moment; he seemed to consider it.

"Certain parts of the past you don't want to see," he said finally.

"Why is that?"

"Too painful."

"Too painful happy — or too painful sad?"

"Too painful happy," he said, without a moment's hesitation.

"Really."

I considered that for a moment. Then I asked:

"How old will we look? — Forty? Twenty?"

"We'll look to be of an uncertain age," Art said. "A little like those people who age well — whose age is difficult to guess. For the most part we'll look like we did then — again, maybe slightly older... this holds true except, well, if you go back farther in time, of course, to childhood, then it's different — then something else happens..."

"What?" I said.

As I asked this, however, he had already turned and disappeared down the basement stairs. I followed him down. The basement smelled damp and earthy, as always.

Art went on: "Also, reason number nine on your list won't work." It was the one about photography, and taking pictures. "It just doesn't work — sorry. You have to leave your cameras behind..."

He was bending over his machine.

"Why?" I said.

He ignored me. "Before I throw the switch," he said, "go upstairs and look out the window. I want you to see something."

We were standing near the foot of the stairs. I was preparing myself for the long — or as he called it, the short — voyage into the year 1969. I went back up the stairs again and stopped at the top.

"Out the living room window, or what?" I called down.

"Yeah," he said. "The living room window. Look under

the elm tree out front."

"Okay," I said, "I'm watching."

I went to the window, pulled back the drapes and looked out across the lawn at the elm tree which was spreading its limbs halfway over the quiet suburban street. It was spring and it was just starting to bud. I didn't know what I was supposed to be looking for. I kept my eyes on the elm tree.

Suddenly, as I watched, a puff of smoke appeared — like something out of a stage-magician's act — and then, sitting at the curb under the tree was a new, polished, silver-colored 1966 Plymouth Satellite with a Hemi engine peeking up through the hood. I knew it was a Hemi engine because this was the car Art had owned — and worked on in his garage — in high school. The rear end was jacked up in the air and there were racing slicks on the back. Poof! — it was amazing — one minute it wasn't there, and the next minute it was. The puff of smoke rose slowly in the air and drifted away through the trees.

I heard Art's footsteps coming up the basement stairs.

"Pretty neat trick, huh?" he said.

"Yeah, Art," I said. "I have to admit it — not bad."

We both looked at it together.

"I'm guessing this means we've arrived," I said, "and that it's there because that's where it was sitting in 1969, am I right?"

"You're catching on already." His eyes were excited. "Want to go for a trip, Nick? Want to ride up to Madison and see what the old town looks like?"

"Sure," I said.

We headed out of town — with Art driving — out past the hospital and the water tower and the Alphorn Lounge, over the ridge of the highway. We passed the population sign, and the sign at the outskirts of town with the little emblems all over it — seals of the Rotary, the Kiwanis, Elks, Moose, and another smaller sign tacked on underneath it that said: "1965 State Basketball Champs," and suddenly we were plunging northward. Art touched the gas pedal a couple of times and we were going about 75.

"Let's not get killed before we even get there, Art," I suggested. Even here, on the smooth asphalt of the main highway, the ride felt bumpy. I hadn't ridden in a car like this in years. It felt like it had no shock absorbers, and my teeth felt like they were shaking loose from their foundations. We were sitting in the not-very-comfortable white naugahyde bucket seats and there was a fire extinguisher on the floor at our feet and a partial roll-bar behind the seats. The car was set up for racing. We could have driven directly down to Daytona and they would have waved us right onto the track.

Art turned toward me, shouting to be heard over the noise: "Isn't this great?!" he said.

The back seat, of course, was nonexistent — in keeping with the conventions of the time — it was ripped out and in its place was a pile of car parts, along with a bunch of tools which were bouncing all over the place. On the highway up to Madison we passed the usual signs advertising farm machinery and seed corn. The sun was out, brilliantly, it was a beautiful spring day, and farm fields on either side were making the transition from the rust-colored brown of winter to a budding soft green. There was a haze hanging over the fields.

A half hour later we had downshifted into a more sane driving mode, going slower, and the roar of the Hemi engine had lessened somewhat. We could finally talk again without shouting. We were a mile or so outside of Madison, bumping along on a frontage road.

It was not like traveling through time at all — I was to feel this sensation more than once — it was more like traveling

forward in space *toward* something... toward a party, maybe —
like going to a party with old friends, seeing the party far-off
on the horizon and hearing the distant laughter of it, and feeling it get closer and closer, more hearty and raucous, and with
this kind of warm feeling... I don't know how else to describe
it... an internal feeling of easy and carefree laughter of youth.
It hurt a little, in some vague, undefined way.

We rode along. For a few minutes neither of us spoke.

"Art, something's troubling me," I said finally.

"Yeah, what's that?"

"This thing about, you don't appear in the future so
something must happen to you. That's not a good sign, is it?"

He signaled to make a right turn and said:

"No."

"In other words, you don't make it into the future and
neither does your machine, that's what you're saying."

"Yeah."

"Well, my question is... how do you know that?"

There was a silence. After what seemed like a long
time, he said quietly:

"I just know."

"Why don't you go ahead into the future a few years
and find out for sure?"

Art smiled slyly. "I did."

"And?"

He shrugged. "Simple... I'm not there."

"You're not there?"

"Not a trace. But I was half-expecting that, in a way.
That's not the odd part."

I looked out the windshield on the right side at some
buildings I hadn't seen in thirty years.

"Okay, what's the odd part?"

"The odd part is, if I go ahead in time like you suggest,
then my entire house is empty, but in my room, everything is
just like I left it... papers, books, notebooks, everything."

"Like a few months later, you mean?"

"Like ten years later."

"Ten years later and nothing has changed in your room?"

He turned and looked at me. "Yeah. But everything else in the house is gone. Strange isn't it?"

I shrugged. "Maybe you're still there — maybe you're still using your room..."

"Nothing ever moves. It's always in the same place."

Art looked out the front windshield, concentrating on driving, his hand on the black eight-ball of a gearshift lever, downshifting. He said nothing.

"And suppose you go ahead twenty years in time..." I said, "then what happens?"

"The same thing. Empty house, but everything in my room stays the same." He looked at me. "What do you suppose would account for something like that?"

"I can't imagine," I said.

We both thought it over for a moment as we looked out the front windshield.

"Front yard mowed?" I asked.

"Yeah."

"Any real estate signs out front?"

"No."

"But the house is empty."

"Yeah."

"Maybe you become so famous," I suggested, "that it's like Independence Hall in Philadelphia or something — where they rope it off and preserve it forever."

Art looked over at me and smiled crookedly.

"I don't think so," he said. "For one thing, it's not roped off. For another — there's no visitors. For a third — they leave my clothes on the floor?"

"They want to keep the natural look — you know, authentic-looking," I said. "The way it was when you were there."

"Right," he said. He had his tongue firmly in his cheek, glancing over at me.

Finally I said:

"Your mother's gone?"

He sighed. "Yeah. Along with all the furniture." He downshifted again and looked over at me. "Except in my room..."

"Well, why don't you work backwards in time, somehow, until you find out what happened?" I suggested, "It might be interesting to know."

There was a long pause. He signaled to make a left-hand turn. The signal light clicked on and off.

"I don't think I want to know," he said finally. "I've thought about it. Something must have happened. A room doesn't sit in a house for twenty years with papers and clothes in it and never change."

We bumped along. The streets had some very large, very deep, spring-time pot-holes. We were entering the outskirts of Madison now. Certain newer buildings that I was expecting to see were missing. Several large shopping malls were also missing. There was vacant land in their place. Old landmarks were still there, of course, but the older buildings looked slightly newer. Also, the town itself seemed to have shrunk inward — to have pulled in its outer boundaries. It was fascinating. Entering the city limits, some of the outer roads that I was familiar with weren't even there. The town seemed to begin farther in, closer toward its center. Everything looked smaller somehow, too, less hectic — as though a third of the population had been removed from the town, mainly from the outskirts. The traffic was much less than I was familiar with in modern day. It was rather pleasant — almost quaint. It had more of an innocent, small-town quality. It was amazing to see.

I happened to look down at one point, instinctively, at my watch, and the hair rose on the back of my neck. It was an old watch I was wearing — one I'd worn a long time ago, and hadn't seen for many years. This single event struck me with great feeling for some reason. I looked at it suddenly with great fondness — seeing it again. It was like seeing an old friend... And also the shirt I was wearing too. I suddenly noticed it with astonishment... It was a great old shirt — a wonderful faded, blue work shirt that I used to wear all the time back then... I remembered how I had loved that shirt, and hadn't seen *it* for years either. Looking at it, you couldn't help but wondering where all these things go over the years... Where has that wrist-watch been since then? Was it in a landfill somewhere? It made you wonder where the small stuff goes — things you use every day, without ever thinking about them. And then one day they disappeared, piece by piece, and were silently replaced. Now, of course, seeing it, I remembered it well. I had worn it for years... I panicked suddenly and immediately grabbed for my wallet. Art laughed.

"The stuff in your pockets will be the same," he answered.

"Why is that?"

He smiled, and shrugged. "I never figured that out," he said.

"And why are my shoes the same, but my pants and shirt are different?"

He shrugged again. "Again I don't know. Some kind of cosmic joke — a blend of the two eras maybe—" He laughed again.

I stared down at my pair of new, bright-colored running shoes, looking at them curiously. Then I also noticed something else. I had had some minor back problems over the years. It was nothing serious but I could occasionally feel it. Yet now it felt different somehow — younger and stronger. All the usual minor twinges of pain were missing.

We drove down Monroe Street, turned on Johnson and finally onto Park Street, and Art let me off at the corner of State and Park, in front of the university campus. The older buildings of the University looked pretty much the same. A few of the modern touches were missing. The campus mall was also missing — with its array of trees and lights and benches — and in its place was just a street, with traffic. I talked to Art for a moment at the car window before setting off alone on my mission to find Ida. It had sounded like a great adventure, a great epic quest when we talked about it — now it just seemed like an ordinary day. It didn't seem like a different year at all.

It didn't *feel* like it either. Except for certain changes in the landscape — which you quickly got used to — it seemed like any other kind of trip... in space, not time.

"Good luck in your search," Art said.

"Good luck in yours, Art," I said back to him.

He stuck his hand out the window and I shook it firmly. He reached down for the gearshift knob and prepared to go.

"Anything I should know?" I asked.

"It's all pretty self-explanatory," he said. "You'll get along just fine. It'll be easy. You'll be surprised."

"And I'll meet you where?"

"At Rennebohm's, on State Street."

"Just out of curiosity," I said to him through the window, "You know that one time when you went ahead into the future?"

"Yeah?"

"You didn't happen to see me around anywhere, did you?"

Art laughed out loud at this. It struck him funny. "I never went out of the house, Nick," he said. "Sorry."

5

The past is a foreign country; they do things differently there.
— L.P. Hartley

It was no problem finding Ida. In the late Sixties she was living in a commune on the outskirts of Madison — a hotbed of anti-war activity at the time — with about twenty other people. I knew where to find her, yes. The Hog Farm, it was called — after its more famous namesake in California. I took a cab out there, marveling at the interior of the ancient taxi.

Ida. Probably every man has an Ida in his background somewhere. She was the genuine article — intense, passionate, spontaneous, unpredictable. Gypsy-like. And one might also add: off-the-chart, go-for-broke sexuality. She was the one that could snap you out of the general overall boredom of life and make you come alive — pull you right on through that dull plane of everyday existence. She danced to her own music, Ida did. In my memory she was like a gypsy dancer outside a traveling covered-wagon in the firelight — dancing by herself, to a tune only she could hear, and in a very erotic way too... (This was my memory of her, and I was about to find out if it was true.) But not... and this was important too... not an imitation of these things. It wasn't a show she was putting on for someone else or anything like that. It was instinctive with her, built-in and bone-deep. And so I had to see her again. Now that it was possible, the desire became more intense. Was she like I remembered? I had to find out. It was the one reason I couldn't resist Art's invitation. And as I say, I knew where to find her.

I use the metaphor of the gypsy caravan and the firelight because that is very close to the way I found her. It was that night — the night after Art had left me off, about 10 p.m., and they were sitting around a campfire out of doors, all the members of this Sixties commune. They were visible from a distance as I approached, walking through an open field toward the Hog Farm. My nerves were on edge; I could hear the husks of broken cornstalks crunching under my feet as I walked.

The firelight was reflecting in all their faces, sitting in a circle, as I came up. I said hello as softly as I could, but coming out of the darkness, they were startled by my approach.

"It's a narc," someone said in a low, uneasy voice.

"Yeah, like he's going to admit it, man, if he is," someone else answered him.

"I'm not a narc," I said, in what I hoped was my softest, most reassuring voice.

"He doesn't look like a narc," someone else said, to scattered laughter.

There was a pause while they looked me over in the firelight.

"He doesn't dress like a narc," someone added.

More laughter.

"I'm a friend of Ida's," I said. "She around?"

"Nick!" I heard a voice say then, that familiar voice from long ago, out of my past, and one of the forms emerged from the circle and stood up in the dark and ran toward me. It was Ida all right. She was dressed in a long peasant dress. An instant later I was being held in the firm tug of her embrace.

This went on for a moment or two, and then she pulled back and held me at arm's length. "Nick, what are you doing here?" she said excitedly, "I thought you were in... Chicago. You said you were going to Chicago—"

I shrugged, trying to sound casual.

"I decided to come back," I said.

"Hey, man, good to see you," someone within the circle stuck out his hand, "Any friend of Ida's... Take a seat: we were just grooving on the fire."

An outstretched arm extended toward me, from out of the group. It held a long Indian-type pipe sculpted out of wood, with a handful of long feathers hanging down from the sides.

God, I was looking into the face of Ida. I couldn't be-lieve it. And I couldn't take my eyes off her. The firelight shone on her face. There it was all over again, the green flash of her eyes, the energy, the youth — now I remembered it — it all came back, the great energy she had... She took both my hands and looked directly into my eyes. I could feel her gaze flicker back and forth hungrily across my face, absorbing me. She was good at that — looking at you directly, full force. But now she said, with uncertainty, and a quizzical smile: "Say some-thing, Nick. What's the matter? Are you stoned?"

"No," I said. "I... I'm just..."

"Well, I'm... like, real surprised," she said. "I didn't think you were ever coming back, the way you talked... Why, the last time we talked you said..."

She let it trail off.

There was certain puzzlement in her tone. I couldn't remember what I'd told her.

"I guess I just changed my mind, Ida," I said. "I had to see you one more time..."

She kept looking into my eyes. At the same time she took me by the hand and drew me over to where she had been sitting by the campfire. There was an opening in the circle of people and we both sat down, cross-legged. The campfire blazed before us, popped and crackled hypnotically. Everyone around the circle was looking at it in a glazed, somnambulent fashion. Nobody was paying much attention to me. Ida put her arm around me as we sat down, oblivious to any of the others, and soon after that she was kissing me; I could feel her breathing change. "It's so good to see you, Nick," she said. From time to time she stopped and looked up at me, into my eyes, as if searching for something there. Very direct, I thought, that was Ida. You had to grab life with her, physically. Every step of the way she charmed you, seduced you... I had been here, what, five minutes, and we had already just *eased* into love-making — as if it were the most natural thing in the world. I could feel Ida's bones and arms and sinews straining toward me.

The group was in the process of passing the marijuana pipe around the circle, and finally, after saying no a couple of times, I gave in. The pipe made a couple more passes and several tokes later my vision shifted and my eyes became narrowed and disoriented and the world became a fragmented place, like a mirror cut into two planes that I was unable to fit together. After that it was all back: the Sixties. I gazed, like them, at the fire — unable to take my eyes off it. In the reflected glow of the flames people sitting around in the circle suddenly became ancient warlocks in a primitive tribe, striving toward some higher plane — that cosmic effort everyone was so involved in back then.

"Nick, I... well, even seeing you, I still don't believe it," Ida said, looking at me, "You just walked out of the dark like that... But God, it's so good to see you." Her hand was on my leg, softly. She seemed unable to take her eyes off me, and I, for my part, couldn't take my eyes off her. It was like we hadn't seen each other for a hundred years, which, in a certain sense, we hadn't.

They were telling stories around the fire now and that's when, probably because I was getting stoned myself, I got careless and let my guard down. Well, I had an excuse — they started quizzing me: "Where you from stranger? Where do you hail from?" That sort of thing. Also, there were those around the campfire who, in an exaggerated spirit of transcendentalism and psychedelia, were making some mighty big claims.

"I'm Diana, Huntress of the moon," one was saying, for instance.

Oh really, I thought.

"I have been in time and space," said the voice of another young woman in the circle, her face aglow in the firelight — moving her hands and arms rhythmically, to unseen music.

"I am Pisces," said a third.

I remembered how this went, of course, I knew the drill. I knew what they were driving at, but I also knew where they were going, and what the next phase in their lives would be, and how this would all become a part of their past. About the third time they asked me, I joined in the celebration of exaggerated hyperbole, and I let it slip out.

"I'm from the future," I heard my voice announce.

At first — I was a little surprised — there was no reaction at all. They all seemed to take it completely in stride. Oh, he's from the future. Hey, cool. Far out.

There was silence for a moment, and then a man's voice said, "We have here among us a visitor from the far future."

There wasn't any sarcasm to it. That was the surprising part. There wasn't any skepticism — just a straightforward statement of fact.

"Speak, man of the far future," said the voice again, "Tell us of your wisdom."

"Well, I wouldn't call it the far future," I said modestly, "Just the 1990's."

This brought another short spell of silence. The wind in the trees was the only sound. A couple of them leaned forward then, listening, nodding in hippie-like fashion. Ida was looking at me with her mouth parted slightly now, like I had lost my mind. She was nestled into me, though, and her face shone wonderfully in the firelight as she gazed up at me. The expression on her face said: "Were you smoking something before you got here, Nick?"

"Yeah, it's not what I'd call the far future," I repeated,

into the silence. "In fact, it's not that far off, really, if you think about it — though I suppose it seems like it is to you..."

I could feel a change then, in the attitudes around the campfire. People were shifting in their places. There was a clearing of throats. Someone handed me a bottle of ripple wine they were passing around.

After another pause, without skipping a beat, the first man spoke again.

"Tell us of the world of the 1990's, oh, traveler," he said. "In that far-off year when there will be no more pollution, no more automobiles, no more war, no more disease. When a wiser people will have emerged, with leaders of wisdom..."

"I don't want to disappoint you," I said to him, "But in that far-off year things won't be a whole lot different than they are right now — except maybe the cars will be a little smaller and there's a lot more TV channels."

This caused another deafening silence.

By this time, a look of deep and serious concern had come over Ida's face.

"What's the matter with you, Nick?" she whispered, under her breath, "Are you okay?"

"A little stoned," I said. "I'm fine."

Now there was growing curiosity around the campfire. Okay. I had let it slip out. Did it matter? What would Art say? He hadn't said not to tell anyone, did he? I couldn't remember. Maybe it didn't matter.

The cosmic psychedelic tone was falling away now, among the crowd, and common garden-variety curiosity was starting to take its place.

"And in these far future days," said an inquiring voice, "who will be our President?"

"Well, there's going to be several of them you don't know about — Reagan, Bush, Clinton..."

This was a stopper. If they weren't interested before, I definitely had their attention now. It suddenly seemed like nobody was breathing but me. The fire popped and crackled. The wind blew. Somebody turned off a radio. Every eye in the night was on me.

"Not Governor Reagan from California?" one voice asked with amazement, and a hint of derision, "Governor Ray-guns? It's not possible—"

There was some laughter around the campfire.

"Yeah, it's quite possible," I said, and took another swig of wine from the bottle being passed around. I added, cryptically: "Remember, you heard it here first."

"Reagan..." said the first man, repeating the name, dumbstruck.

"Yeah. Governor Reagan — one and the same," I said. "But don't worry, it turned out all right, more or less. I mean, he didn't blow up the world or anything."

There was more dead silence around the campfire.

I went on: "What I'm saying is, they're not carving his face on Mount Rushmore or anything like that, but the country survived it, more or less—"

I could see varying levels of astonishment in the faces around the fire.

"How could something like that happen?" one of them asked skeptically, and I sat racking my brain trying to explain it, in a way that would make sense from their point of view.

"How did it happen?" I said. "Well, it happened in the usual way... he got in the race, he won more primaries than anyone else, and then he won the general election. He beat, let's see, Carter...? Carter happened to be low in the ratings at the time because of that hostage thing..."

They were all looking at me, a circle of faces in the firelight.

"Who's Carter?" somebody else asked.

"He's a guy from Georgia — a soft-spoken guy with a drawl and a big smile..." I said. "I think he might be governor of Georgia now, something like that, you can look it up..."

There was another short, stunned silence.

"So you're saying Ronald Reagan gets to be President," one of them said, shaking his head. "I knew it — I knew the world was going to hell."

"Well, actually a guy named Bill Clinton is President now... He came after Bush, who was vice-president under Reagan for eight years..."

The same silence and puzzlement greeted this statement.

"Bill Clinton?" one of them said.

"Yeah, he's a Democrat," I explained, "In the 60's he was kind of a hippie — against the war."

"Great!" someone yelled.

"But he doesn't look like a hippie in the 1990's."

"What does he look like?"

"He looks like an insurance salesman."

"And what happens to the anti-war movement then?" another voice asked. I could detect further skepticism, even hostility.

I said: "Hey, don't get mad at me — I didn't cause this stuff to happen. The anti-war movement... I don't know, it just fizzled out."

This wasn't the answer they were looking for, but it couldn't be helped. I was beginning to wish, not for the only time, that I knew my history better.

I said: "The Vietnam War ended, peace was declared, the troops came home, and the anti-war movement fizzled out..." I shrugged "—end of story..."

They all stared. Indian chiefs in the 1800's couldn't have been more deadpan.

I added, to fill in the silence: "There was a short war a few years ago. Against Iraq. We won. It didn't last very long. We had a lot of modern, hi-tech weapons."

"Iraq," someone said numbly, weakly.

"Yeah — but they were really asking for it."

"The thing about him is, he sounds so definite," said a woman's voice, "With such certainty."

"And what else happens in this future?" asked another voice, skeptically.

I shrugged. "I don't know, the usual stuff... All the same stuff that happens in any year... you know."

I could tell they didn't know. I could tell from their

faces. Someone handed me a large jug of Sangria wine that had now been opened and had succeeded the Ripple being passed around the circle. I took a gulp of it, wiped my mouth on my sleeve, and waited for the next question. I knew it was coming.

"Anything else happen?"

I said, "Let's see... well, it's hard to remember." I thought it over for a moment. "You know, things change... but they happen gradually, so you don't really notice them. And then you get used to them — they're no big deal after awhile and you forget about them—"

I looked around at their faces. They had no idea what I was talking about. They looked at me like I was babbling. Maybe I was.

I tried to think, again. My brain was not operating at its best. I hadn't been stoned in about twenty-five years, and it was not helping my thinking process. I took a deep breath and said: "Let me think... the Viet Nam War got over in, what year was it — 1973, something like that. I don't remember how it got over, really. It just did — it ended. It wound down — then it stopped. Reagan retired from office in about, what... '88? Which means he must have been elected in 1982..." I was working backwards, trying to remember the dates. I was terrible at history. I wished again I would have boned up on it a little. By this time Ida had pulled away from me too, and had — psychologically speaking — joined the group, all of whom were staring, sitting with their jaws dropped open.

"Well, who was President before Reagan then?" someone else asked.

I said: "Why, Nixon was, of course. No, wait — Carter was. Yeah, Carter was in between — he came after Nixon and Ford... when Nixon resigned..."

"Nixon resigned?" one of them said.

"Yeah, in 1974."

Hearing this, a sudden cheer went up around the campfire.

I had them now. As an audience, I had them.

"Why'd he resign?"

"Why?" I repeated. I glanced up in the air. "Why'd Nixon resign... Well, it was kind of complicated, and here again, I just can't remember it all. It had something to do with this burglary at this hotel — the Watergate hotel in Washington, where the Democrats had their offices or something, and Nixon gave the okay for it or something... I don't know exactly the... I'm not a historian," I explained. "They were getting ready to impeach him, though..."

"Far out," someone said, with feeling.

"What else?" asked another voice, hungrily.

"What else?" I said. I now wished I had never brought any of this up — wished to get out of this conversation altogether, and just sit back and close my eyes. Remembering, I added: "Oh, there is a plague..."

"A plague!" someone said. If all eyes weren't on me before, they were now.

"It's called AIDS. It started about... well, it started about now, actually. In the late Sixties. For a long time nobody knew what it was. In fact, that's one of the reasons I'm here..."

Several people had moved away from me — an inch or two — after I'd said this, as if I'd said that I had the Bubonic Plague. Ida's eyes were as big as saucers now. I was beginning to be real sorry I had brought any of this up. I hadn't meant to mention any of it...

"No, no, it's not like that," I assured them, "It's not like that at all... It's sexually transmitted. It's like... syphilis, you know, that sort of thing. Or if you take drugs with needles. That kind of thing. Otherwise, you can't get it."

Later, the gathering broke up and Ida and I sat by the fire alone — everyone else had gone to bed — a couple of them stopped by and shook my hand on the way out, saying, "Nice rap, man." They shook my hand in the old hippie handshake — high up, with emphasis on the thumb — and then the embers burned low, and Ida and I sat on for awhile. She was still speechless, looking at me. Finally we retired to her tent nearby. Several of the commune members were sleeping outdoors under the night sky in sleeping bags; it was a warm spring night. The stars were out overhead in the heavens.

Ida was wearing her long peasant-type dress which she quickly drew up over her head, and, after a short educational discussion on my part concerning the merits of Safe Sex, the next half hour was spent in rapturous pleasure of the kind I thought I'd never experience again — a blur of soft white skin outlined in the reflections of candlelight inside the tent. The book on Ida was that she made love to you — not the other way around. That hadn't changed. Love-making was like a physical sport with her — involving muscles and exertion and effort and energy. The candlelight made exaggerated shadows, and silhouettes moved on the walls of the tent as her lithe form shone above me, gleaming softly in the light. Behind her, and above her, these monstrous apparitions hovered on the roof of the tent. I remembered it now — it was all coming back — a kind of aggressive, hungry, bone-crunching sexuality. I had never known a woman with more energy, I thought. I had known more beautiful women, perhaps, but none with her passion and intensity. She was fierce, in a way, as if hungry for experience. After what seemed like an hour of exhausting activity we dragged her sleeping bag outside, along with some blankets, and stretched out under the night sky where we lay together looking up at the stars. I had never seen the heavens as clear as they were on this night, the stars so brilliant. All the constellations were visible... the Big Dipper, the Little Dipper, clearly outlined in their connect-the-dot fashion across a black velvet background. Ida gazed up at them too, her arms behind her head.

"What was all that back there, Nick?" she asked finally. You could tell she'd been saving up the question. "All that 'I'm from the future' stuff?"

She wanted to know but she still had a slight smirk on her face as she said it — her merry, youthful, flirtatious Ida-smirk. Before I could answer, though, she rolled over toward me quickly, and said: "I don't care where you came from Nick, really — I don't care if you came from the future, from Mars, or from Chicago — it's just good to have you back."

"What exactly did I say to you when we broke up?" I asked her suddenly, dying to know.

She thought for a second. "What did you say? We had an argument — don't you remember? — about who would call who up on the phone. It was stupid really."

"*That's* why we broke up?"

"Yeah. You said you'd call me and then you never called, so... I decided not to call you either. Silly wasn't it?"

I sat and wondered. She said, "Let's forget about all that and do it again."

"Do what again?"

"What do you think?" She whispered in my ear: "You know, make love again" — her eyes flashing, challenging me. The idea had suddenly come to her, the way all ideas did with Ida. "Let's do it under the stars..." she gestured upwards, toward the heavens.

"I don't think so, Ida," I said.

"Why?"

"I'm too tired."

She rolled over again, mildly irritated, and said:

"You're too tired?"

"Yeah, I'm too tired," I said. "We just made love about five minutes ago."

She gave an imitation of a pout. There was a long pause.

Finally she said: "All that stuff about the future — were you putting them on back there, or what?" She smiled a little; the thought of it amused her.

"Yeah, I was putting them on."

She looked at me.

"Well, you were doing a pretty damn good job of it," she said. "They were all buying it..."

She lay on her back now, holding up the stalk of some

plant she had found nearby, picking at it. Beyond her on the horizon the winking stars were a backdrop.

I watched her. She looked incredibly beautiful laying there. Her sleeping-bag only reached halfway up, and her breasts were visible, flattened by gravity. She didn't notice, or care.

I looked at her and suddenly started thinking about Art then, wondering about him and where he was and if he was all right. And that made me start thinking about AIDS again.

"Who have you made love to lately, Ida?" I asked her suddenly.

She shifted around, got herself up on one elbow and looked at me.

"Oh, everyone," she said.

I let out a sigh.

"That's terrific," I said.

"Why?"

"Why?" I said. "Didn't you hear what I said back there? There's a plague starting... a sexual plague... I mean, for all I know it's probably still safe, but, God Ida..."

She smiled her beatific smile; her face glowed. *Lucy In The Sky With Diamonds*... It was going to be hopeless, I thought. She looked beautiful — absolutely, fabulously beautiful — the way you only look once, at a certain time in your life. Wonderfully, sublimely erotic — like a vision of a Victorian waif. Or a young flapper at the height of the 1920's. She was every young hippie of the '60's at their best, most innocent moment. Yes, it was going to be hopeless. Her eyes gleamed and she stretched her arms above her head, far as they would go, as if reaching for the stars. Then she turned and reached out again for me. "Are you ready yet?" — insistently, hungrily.

"No, Ida," I said. "I'm not ready yet... I'm worn out, actually. Don't you ever get tired? Ever?"

There was another long pause at this. She looked again at the plant stalk and picked at it with her fingers.

"So you're from the future, Nick," she said. She smiled to herself. Then she laughed out loud suddenly. "God, and all this time I thought you were in Chicago." She laughed again at her joke.

"Very funny, Ida," I said.

"I suppose everybody in the future wears these stream-lined futuristic clothes — like in 'Star Trek'..." She was still looking at the plant stalk.

"No, actually, they wear the same clothes people wear now — blue-jeans and T-shirts..."

"Really."

"Yes, really. Now, Ida..." I began.

She interrupted me — faced me quickly, getting an idea. Everything happened quickly with Ida. "Suppose you were, Nick," she said eagerly, "Suppose you *were* from the future — Wow, think of it — wouldn't it be exciting?"

"Yeah," I said.

She drew a deep breath and let out a long sigh. She stared up at the stars again.

"By the way, if you're from the future," she said, "they must have some fabulous music there, eh?"

"Oh, they've got their share of clinkers, believe me."

"Anything as good as the Beatles?" she said. "I bet no-body remembers the Beatles anymore..."

"Twenty-five years later?" I said with some irritation, "They don't remember the Beatles twenty-five years later? Think for a second, Ida..."

"Oh — I guess you're right. But I bet they never play them anymore."

"They play the Beatles all the time," I said. "Every day, almost..."

She looked skeptical. "Oh, sure they do..." she said.

"They play them just about every day," I said, "—on the radio."

"Oh sure, they play the Beatles every day in the 1990's," she laughed, "Tell me another one." Nothing could have seemed more unlikely to her.

"Well, they don't play them every goddamn song, no," I said. "But they get their fair share of air-time. There's oldies radio stations and—"

"In the future everybody wears T-shirts and blue jeans and they play the Beatles on the radio all the time," she said with a chuckle. "Tell me another one."

"That's slightly oversimplifying it," I said.

"You make it sound a lot like now."

"Well it is a lot like now."

There was a moment's silence.

"Did they break up?" — quickly, with a cocked eyebrow — like it was a test question.

"Break up?"

"The Beatles. A fan magazine said they were going to break up."

"Yeah," I said. "They broke up."

She thought about that. A small frown crossed her face.

"Did they ever get back together?"

"No," I said.

"Too bad."

"John died," I said. "That's one reason."

This stopped her — cold. "John *died?*" she said, turning slowly toward me, her jaw open. It knocked the air out of her. "He died? What of?"

"Some guy shot him. In about 1980 or so, something like that — I forget the exact year."

"You're kidding—"

"No, I'm not kidding."

"Where did it happen?" she asked, in disbelief.

"In New York," I said.

"In New York, God... I mean... who did it?"

"Some low-life," I said. "The name escapes me right now."

"But you seem so... so... calm about it, so matter-of-fact.."

"Ida, I said I was from the 1990's, didn't I?"

"Yeah..."

"Well then that would mean that to me it happened a long time ago, wouldn't it?"

"Yeah, I guess so."

She thought about it.

Then she sat up, suddenly, getting an idea.

"What?" I said.

"We've got to warn him," she said. "We've got to tell him."

I hadn't thought of that. "Well, yeah, I suppose you're right," I said. "Not that he's going to listen to us or take it seriously." I pictured myself calling up John Lennon on the phone and telling him that ten years or so from now some guy with a handgun was going to come looking for him, so don't be giving out any autographs on that particular day. Right, uh-huh. I pictured the phone going dead in my hand.

"I know," Ida said, with a new idea, "We could write him a letter." Then she stopped again, suddenly. "Hey, wait a minute," she said. The skeptical look returned again. She was getting drawn into it — the whole thing — and she had suddenly realized it and caught herself. I saw her expression change.

"Gees, you know, I'm getting worried about you, Nick — I mean, seriously, where are you getting all this from? It's scary... Have you been dropping acid?"

"No," I said.

She looked at me for a long time, her head cocked to one side. Just looking, as if she couldn't figure me out. Finally she sighed and collapsed back down on the sleeping bag, spread her arms out to either side like a crucifix, and looked up at the stars one more time. Her body had a pale, marble-white aspect under the moonlight.

"The future, huh?" she said and laughed.

"Yeah," I said, and laughed.

"Sing me a song from the future," she said suddenly, in a dreamy voice. The entranced, romantic look had returned. "Sing me a song from the future, Nick."

"Yeah?" I said.

"Yeah," she said. It was another test. Smirking, daring me, challenging me.

"I don't know... I'm not very good at music, Ida. You

know that. I don't remember..." I could see the highly skeptical look return, so I tried to think of something. Finally I began to sing, in a low voice, the song *Every Breath You Take* by the Police. It was an old song, but it was the first song that came to mind. It was probably not a great choice either — it was not the kind of song you sing solo, and it needed a bass real bad, which I tried to supply with intermittent humming, but she listened in rapt fascination.

Her eyes were excited and alive, and something else, too — very merry, very amused.

"God, it's not bad," she said. "Really. If you just made that up, it's not bad. It's kind of catchy, actually..."

I sang another line or two from the song.

"What year is it from?"

"I don't remember... early Eighties, 1982, 1983, something like that."

"Something like that," she said, mimicking me, "Just offhand — early Eighties..."

I laughed.

"Got any other ones?" she said with great interest.

"Let's see..." I said. I thought a moment and then sang a few bars of the song by U2: *I Still Haven't Found What I'm Looking For.* After that I did a minor rendition of *Heart of Glass* by Blondie and a little bit of *Margaritaville* by Jimmy Buffett — as much as I could remember — and a few chords from the Bob Seger song, *Against the Wind.* Finally I wrapped it up with a few stanzas of the song, *Candle In The Wind* by Elton John:

"Goodbye, Norma Jean, though I never knew you at all..."

She was turned to the side and had her chin resting in her hand, watching me, listening with fascination.

"...It seems to me, that you lived your life, like a candle in the wind... never knowing who to turn to, when the rains came... Your candle burned out long before, your legend ever did..."

The song seemed appropriate — it described Ida to a T.

"Who's that by?" she asked.

"Elton John," I said.

"Odd name," she said.

"Yeah."

"Who's Norma Jean?"

"Marilyn Monroe," I said. "That was her real name."

"Hmm." She paused. Then she said, almost wistfully: "Are the Rolling Stones still around?"

"Yeah, sure. Except they're a lot older."

She laughed at this. I watched her unzip the zipper of her sleeping bag, then a moment later she was stepping out and standing in the night, standing over me, and a moment after that she was wrapping us both up in the blankets. Underneath the blankets it was warm and comfortable and I felt the body-length sensation of her skin against mine, soft and smooth in the night. In the distance I could hear the sound of a dog barking, and faraway also, from a radio, the sounds of a song by Creedence Clearwater Revival.

In the morning the sun was up and I awoke to the smell of coffee brewing and a sore back from sleeping on the hard, lumpy ground. As a matter of fact, I hurt all over. Ida was standing over me holding a cup of coffee in one hand and a coffee pot in the other, looking down at me. Other commune members were busying themselves nearby, doing chores. The morning sky seemed wide, blue, sunny and very bright.

"Wake up, sailor," Ida said. She waved the coffee pot at me, "Have a rough night?"

"Yes," I said. "I had a rough night." She laughed. I had forgotten what a marvelous laugh she had.

I stretched a little, not feeling much like getting up. My back hurt. My ribs hurt. It was an unfamiliar feeling waking up out-of-doors. I hadn't done it in a long time. Ida looked as fresh and healthy — of course — as someone returning from a twelve-mile hike. She was wearing a white blouse tied in a knot in the front and a pair of blue jeans, her hair disheveled, but attractively so. She looked spectacular, as always.

I watched as she sat down swiftly, agilely, in cross-legged fashion. She produced a small mirror — one of these round plastic compacts — and began putting on makeup, looking into the mirror-glass very earnestly.

I watched her in silence, saying nothing. God, she was beautiful.

"So, how's the man from the future today?" she asked busily, without looking up.

"He's a little fuzzy and a little hung-over," I said, "and also a little tired."

She was humming to herself. Taking her time. It was a breezy spring day. There were a few clouds in the sky. She had all the time in the world. She clicked and unclicked the compact absently several times, looking past it to the horizon.

"A hangover?" she said, with feigned surprise. "Don't they have cures for that in the future? A miracle pill you take or something?"

"Yes," I said. "It's called aspirin. It comes in little green bottles. Could we drop the subject of the future?"

"All right," she said. She was humming to herself again, taking deep breaths, as if trying to take it all in — the morning, the air, the sunlight — closing her eyes, humming her tune. I couldn't make out the song. Also, I couldn't take my eyes off her. Her hair blew behind her as she sat in the breeze with her knees up, cradled in her arms. I hadn't been around the hippie mode of lifestyle for a long time... there was something alluring about it, somehow, a nice casualness about it, as if time had stopped, as if it was unlimited...

It tempted you. It made you want to go back to a time when Time itself was more open-ended... It made you realize how far you had strayed from it — how *structured* you got later on, how every minute of your day was accounted for, every day of the week — with jobs and family and other obligations... You just didn't feel that same careless sense of freedom anymore.

It made you want to go back to a time when the whole notion of time was pried open again... when the individual day seemed to have an unlimited number of hours in it, longer and more carefree...

Ida looked stunningly beautiful on this day, and so young. I never remembered her looking young. She had always seemed quite old and experienced to me at the time. But she seemed young to me now.

"By the way," she said offhandedly, "I was going to ask: are you married? In this future, I mean?"

I sighed. I took a deep breath before I answered. "Yeah," I said. She opened up the mirror again and looked into it deeply and studiously. "But not to me," she said. She pursed her lips in the mirror, then she clicked the compact and unclicked it several more times. She wouldn't look at me.

"No."

"What's her name?"

"Diane."

She smiled at this, then turned toward me again, like this was the greatest game in the world.

"Any kids?" she asked.

"One — a girl. Listen, Ida," I said, "could we get off this? I'm sorry I even brought it up. I should have kept my big mouth shut about it. It was stupid on my part."

She put her finger up to her cheek. "Well, God, what happens to me then, I wonder?" she said, as if to herself. "What happens to poor Ida in this future?"

"I don't know..." I said. "I'm sorry. Maybe that's one of the things I came back to find out."

"And your wife, Nick — what about her?" she said facetiously, "Aren't you kind of stepping out on her? I mean, by being with me...?"

"We're separated," I said. "Soon to be divorced."

"Oh."

She looked away briefly, toward the horizon, and then she turned to me and cocked her head to the side, finally serious. Her face was solemn, almost angry. All the fun and non-sense had gone out of it. "You know, you're really serious about this, aren't you Nick? I mean, I thought you were making all this stuff up, all this future stuff, but... you really believe it, don't you?" She got to her feet again. She paced around. She threw up her hands. She was working herself up into a good fit now.

"God, I don't know..." she said. "I see you two weeks ago, we have an argument, you walk out of here telling me you may call me, or you may not, and to forward all your mail to some post office box in Chicago. Now you show up three weeks later saying you've been in the future, and frankly, it's not very much different than now, except don't look for any more Beatle albums to come out. Jesus, what am I supposed to think, Nick? Look at it from my point of view..."

"I know it sounds a little odd — I'm sorry, Ida," I said.

She looked at me for a long time then, her hands on her hips, shaking her head from side to side, as if to say I was a lost cause. Her hair shifted back and forth in the breeze. She stood there, backlighted against the sky, and it was just a single moment in time, but it was one of those moments when time seems to stand still. As she stood there, I don't think I had ever seen anyone look so beautiful in my life. Finally she turned and walked off. After about twenty feet she turned back to me and shouted: "I'm pissed, Nick!" Then she walked on. I lay there, alone. My temptation was to crawl back under the sleeping bag and zip it up — escape into the soft eider down, as it were. But then I remembered I had to meet Art.

6

Wednesday morning.

I was supposed to meet Art in front of Rennebohm's drugstore on State Street at noon. I arrived early, to be sure not to miss him — about twenty minutes early, in fact — but 12 o'clock came and went. No Art. Not knowing what else to do, I went across the street to Brown's bookstore and browsed for a while in one of the front aisles, keeping my eye on Rennebohm's across the street. I thumbed through books on antiques, text-books and second-hand paperbacks for a half hour or so, glancing up every now and then, and finally I gave up. I must have heard him wrong, I thought. I must have the day wrong, or the time. I returned to the Hog Farm, spent the afternoon and night with Ida, and returned again the next day. But there was still no Art. No sign of him. I went into Rennebohm's drugstore, sat at the lunch counter and ate a piece of pie, sat another half hour or so drinking coffee and reading the newspaper. After that I sat near the window and glanced out at the street occasionally, watching the people and old cars go by in fascination. Pedestrians passed by wearing clothing I hadn't seen for twenty-five years. The minutes dragged by. I finally gave up again and left. I was starting to get worried.

I returned to the Hog Farm about mid-afternoon, in a state of puzzlement. I was beginning to wonder what would happen to me if I never found Art again. I was looking at the prospect of living my life over again, from the Sixties on. It wasn't such a dire prospect, of course — after all, I knew how it went — and there were even a few changes I was considering making. But at the same time, I'd already done it, and there was something vaguely disheartening about that. There were just some things I didn't feel like going through again.

"Did you find your friend?" Ida asked when I came back. With Ida, it was more of a seduction than a question — as everything always was with Ida — she put both hands on my shoulders and looked into my eyes deeply with her own, the suggestion of great eroticism and physical attraction written there. She was like a book with a main theme and a counter-theme running just underneath the surface. The counter-theme never stopped.

"No," I said.

About a week went by after that, a week of searching for Art in every bar, restaurant, coffee shop and public place in Madison, but there was no sign of him anywhere. I finally was becoming desperate and went to a place I knew on the Capitol Square which investigated missing persons — a small private detective agency — and I hired this guy named Narmer to look for him. I knew about Narmer; I knew how old he would be, and a few other things about him. I somehow pictured this dashing, suave, middle-aged detective when I saw his name on the frosted glass of the office door, but Narmer was different than I imagined. He turned out to be an ordinary-looking guy, kind of stoop-shouldered, with blond hair and a well-worn business suit. He was sitting behind a desk when I walked in, leaned backwards in one of these spring-loaded office chairs with his hands clasped behind his head. He listened to the story about Art and looked me over, and then he took out a fountain pen and uncapped it and wrote down the name and description in a notebook. He had an odd, slightly skeptical look, kind of half-smiling, like there was something funny about it. Otherwise, he just sat there, taking notes, not saying much. Finally he reached into a top drawer and got out a cigarette, put it between his lips and touched a match to it and looked me over some more. I watched a puff of smoke rise into the office air, then break apart. It shouldn't be too hard to track him down, I suggested, he's got this car — a gray-colored Plymouth Satellite with a Hemi engine sticking up through the hood.

Narmer laughed. He turned the cigarette around in his fingers and looked at it. "If I had a dime for every kid in this town with a Plymouth Satellite with a Hemi engine," he said. "I could retire to Florida."

He smiled again.

"This kid a hippie, a runaway — what?"

"No, he's just a... regular guy," I said.

Narmer wrote something down. "How old?" he asked.

I hesitated.

He tilted his head to the side, as if waiting, and said again:

"How old?"

"Thirty-ish..."

Narmer looked at me.

I added: "Also, I can't afford to spend a lot of money on this — so just see what you can do, okay?"

Another week went by after this, with no word. Then one day in the middle of the week I got a call at the Hog Farm from Narmer.

"I found your buddy," he said.

"Where?"

"He's in jail."

"In jail?"

"Yeah. It seems he was in a fight."

"A fight," I repeated.

"Yeah, he took on some big guy over here at—" searching for the name "—Showalter's Strip Joint. You know, a guy his size, you oughta tell he him shouldn't be picking on big guys,

Nick."

"It doesn't sound like him," I said.

"I got the police report right here," Narmer said. "Claims he instigated the fight too. At least according to the witnesses. He apparently started it, bang, right out of the box. It reads like a kind of a knock-down, drag-out affair too — kicking, biting, clothes ripped, the whole works."

"Well, it just doesn't sound like him," I said again, "He's kind of a small, mousy guy, normally."

"Not this time he wasn't," Narmer said.

I didn't say anything to that.

"The name and description match," Narmer said. "If you want to check it out, he's at the City-County Building."

I walked in the first floor entrance of the City-County Building on Carroll Street and went straight up to the reception desk. They sent me along to another deputy, a liaison officer, and a few minutes later I was on my way up to the seventh floor, to a jail cell to see Art. When we got there, however, the cell was empty. The brown-clad deputy seemed as surprised by this development as I was. He looked at a clipboard curiously. He shrugged.

"He's supposed to be in there," he said.

Another officer, similarly dressed, came down the corridor looking into various cells, and the first officer stopped him.

"What happened to the prisoner that was in this cell?" he asked.

"I think they took him over to the hospital," the man answered.

A half hour later I was at Madison General Hospital, walking through the front doors. I asked at the reception desk, then took the elevator to the third floor, inquired at another desk there, and was given the room number. When I found the room, however, just like at the jail, there was no one there — the bed was neatly made, but empty. It hadn't been slept in. I hailed a passing nurse who looked puzzled, just like the deputy had. She stopped an orderly, who said, "They moved him. He's next door." He pointed at the next room down the hall.

The door was ajar and I walked in and there was Art, big as life. He was laying there, propped up, his head with a bandage around the top, and there was a tube coming out of his nose. He was holding an over-sized TV remote control in one hand, looking at a black and white TV in the corner. His features brightened a hundred percent when he saw me.

"How's it going, Art?" I said. "Jesus, you're a hard guy to find."

"Nick," he said, with a voice filled with joy and relief.

"What the hell happened?" I asked him.

"It didn't hurt, Nick," he said. Proud of himself — tough, manly. "It didn't hurt at all. You know, I always thought it hurt when you got hit. You see these guys on TV — crime shows, that sort of thing — you really feel for them when they get hit. But it doesn't hurt, does it Nick?"

"No, Art," I said. "Not really."

He went on: "One minute I was standing there and ka-bam, the next minute I was on the floor. I didn't know what hit me. I was out like a light. I didn't feel a thing. Hell, it didn't even hurt."

"That's great, Art," I said.

"I got in a couple of shots before I went down, too," he added. He clenched a fist and held it up and flexed it. Then he slapped it into the palm of his other hand a couple times. "I feel wonderful," he said.

"Well, you look like shit," I said.

"What — this?" he said, gesturing toward the bandage on his head. He waved it away. "It's nothing. Just a scratch. They'll take off the bandage in a day or two."

He was white as a sheet. All the blood seemed to have drained from his face.

"You look as pale as a ghost, Art," I said to him.

"No, honestly, I feel good, Nick," he said. "I really do. You know, I always considered myself kind of a... wimpy guy, you know, but I held my own in there. I did. I was right in the middle of it for awhile."

"You really mixed it up," I said.

"Yeah," he said.

"Okay, listen," I said. "Did you find him? This Patient Zero guy you were looking for? Is that what this was all about?"

Art brushed this aside with another gesture of his hand. "No," he said. "I found out there was another guy — *before* him. It wasn't him. That's what I've been doing, that's what I've been researching... This other guy was the *real* Patient Zero, he came along before this guy did. Nobody knows that. And I can prove it." He started getting excited, and then he started coughing, and put his hand over his mouth. As he put it down I could see that there seemed to be a tooth missing. The tube going into his nose shook a little.

"This thing goes back farther than they know," Art continued, "This guy, the real guy, came from St. Louis. And before that he was in Africa. I don't know if he was the first one but... I think that's where..." He started coughing again.

I noticed a bruise on the right side of his forehead, and some scratches on his arm.

"So was this the guy you mixed it up with then?" I asked, "at this strip joint? This guy from St. Louis?"

"Yeah," he said, nodding.

"Well—" I said, prompting him, "What were you doing? I mean, they said you jumped the guy... Were you trying to kill him, or put him out of commission, or what?"

Art hesitated for a moment at this.

"No..." he said. "I, well... I thought I might try to talk sense into him, that's all. I confronted him, you know — I said he was leading a promiscuous lifestyle and that he needed to change his ways..."

"I bet that went over good."

"Yeah. He just laughed at me. Gave me a shove and told me to beat it."

"And then you turned around..." I said.

"Yeah, and whacked him," Art said. The manly tone was back.

"And he whacked you back," I reminded him.

"Well... yeah, basically."

There was a moment's silence.

Art played with the TV remote control, fingering it idly, turning it around in his hand.

"By the way," he said finally, "How'd you find me?"

"I hired a guy to look for you."

"Oh," he said.

"Listen, Art," I said finally, "There's something I've got to talk to you about..."

"Sure," he said.

"The thing is, well, it's been on my mind, lately — if something were to happen to you, how would I... get back?"

"Nothing's going to happen to me," he assured me, "You can rest easy on that count."

"Art, you're already in the fricking hospital, and frankly, you don't look so hot... like you could drop dead at any moment, so just hypothetically, tell me what to do, okay?"

Art laughed. "Okay. It's simple, Nick, you just set the switches on my machine the other way — flip them all back like they were. There's a piece of masking tape on the right side with the words written on it, *Madison Retro* — just move the switch over in that direction."

"That's it?" I said.

He shrugged. "Yeah. Actually, there's more to it, but that'll get you out of it."

Well, it seemed simple enough, I thought. Almost too simple. "I just thought I might need to know, that's all," I said.

"Don't worry," Art said. "I'll be around." He laughed, then began coughing again. "Just remember — *Madison Retro*."

"Okay. Can I ask why it's so important?"

"Well, because it's *space specific,*" he said. "It's like a computer. It needs a starting point — geographically speaking..."

"Why is geography important? I thought this was about

Time—"

"Don't worry — it just is."

He said it with such authority that I had to ask:

"What would happen if I got it wrong?"

Art smiled ruefully.

"Let's put it this way," he said. "Have you ever been to Turkey in the 11th Century? Or Calcutta in the 4th Century?"

"Madison Retro," I repeated to myself, "I'll remember."

Art smiled. "Anything else?"

"Yeah, where's the car?" I said. "I need it."

"The cops impounded it, I think," Art said.

"Why would they do that?"

"Because it was double-parked while I was looking for the guy."

"That's great," I said.

I turned to go. Then I remembered one other thing.

"Art, one last thing. Suppose something did happen to you — I mean, just hypothetically speaking — and I didn't change the machine? What would happen? I mean, to me—"

He shrugged. "No big deal. Live it out," he said, "same as you did the first time. You know how it goes. It wasn't that bad, was it?"

"No, I guess not." There was still something troubling about it. It wasn't quite the answer I was looking for. It was like being asked to view a movie you'd already seen — a very *long* movie.

"Also—" Art added, "As long as we're on the subject, I should mention one other thing. If you go back far enough in time, you start to dissemble—"

"What's that mean?"

"Well, it's like... you're in it, living it, but at the same time you're outside yourself, watching it."

"Why is that?"

"Well, because if you went back far enough you'd be a little kid — and there'd be a natural schism between you as an adult and you as a kid."

"Uh-huh."

"The only reason I mention it is because you may be feeling a little of that already, and you may wonder about it."

"All right," I said. "That's the way it works, huh?"

"Yeah." Art nodded to himself.

I watched him try to smile again under the bandages. Then I turned to go.

"Well," I said, "don't die on me, okay?"

Art smiled. "Don't worry, I'm not going anywhere. I'm going to be around for a long, long time." He gave me a thumbs-up signal.

"Sure. That's the spirit," I said.

Afterwards, as I was leaving, I pulled the door shut quietly. Outside in the hallway I encountered the orderly again, standing in a green smock, holding a mop. "I don't think your buddy's going to make it," he said.

7

The lot where the car was impounded was located on the east side of town near where the East Towne shopping mall would be built years later. There was a tall chain-link fence with spikes on top surrounding an open field with forty or fifty parked cars squeezed in, side by side. The field was bordered on two sides with piles of tires and car parts running the whole length of the fence. Sandwiched between all of this junk somewhere, presumably, was Art's car. I gave the paperwork to a soiled-looking young man with an oval face and a drowsy manner and he looked at it indifferently, then waved to another young man inside the fence. The field was hilly and deeply rutted and when I reached the car, it wouldn't start. The second young man saw this and climbed in an old pickup truck with a rubber bumper and pushed Art's Plymouth out of the line of cars, over the mud-rut road and out onto the narrow street in front of the impound lot. Now the car was outside the lot but it still wouldn't start. The man in the pickup truck shouted, "I'll give you another push!" Presently I felt the lurch of the truck hitting my bumper and soon we were moving down the road, picking up speed. A giant gas-tanker pulled out in front of us at one point and I hit the brakes with no effect at all. The kid was still pushing me. We narrowly missed the gas tanker, and a moment later Art's car coughed to life and I heard the familiar and reassuring throaty roar. I drove back into downtown Madison cursing the kid in the pickup all the way.

During the next week I spent more and more time with Ida, falling in love with her all over again. Late one afternoon a couple days later — Art was still in the hospital — I gave the investigator, Narmer, a call.

The phone rang about five or six times, and I was just about to hang up when he picked up the phone.

"Narmer," I said. "It's Nick."

"Nick," Narmer said in a flat, indifferent tone, "What can I do for you?"

"You know that guy you found for me the other day?"

"Yeah — Art."

"Well, I've got a hunch about that fight he was in — have you still got the paperwork from that?"

"Sure."

"How did you go about finding him?"

"In the usual way. Legwork, a few phone calls—"

"Also, I've got a question I'd like to ask you. Mind if I stop up?"

"No, not at all."

I could hear some other noises in the background, like people talking.

"All right," I said. "I'll be over. When's a good time?"

"How about tomorrow? I'll be here."

"Sure. Thanks," I said, and hung up.

Narmer was standing next to an ancient coffee machine with his back to me pouring himself a cup of coffee when I showed up. He had a cigarette dangling out of his mouth. He had an old suit on, and he was wearing a hat. He looked every inch the Philip Marlowe this day.

"Sit down, Nick," he said without looking back.

I took a seat in the chair across from his desk. We talked for a few minutes about Art, and how Narmer had tracked him down, and the fight he was involved in.

"Is that all you wanted to know?" he asked.

"No — I had one other question I wanted to ask you," I said. "It's kind of a detective puzzle. Are you game?"

"Sure. Shoot."

"The question is this: why would a house stand empty for a long time, with no furniture in it, except for one room, which has clothing and books and furniture in it?"

"That's the question?"

"Yeah."

"Is this a real situation?"

"Let's say it is."

Narmer glanced upwards, thinking.

"Who owns the house?"

"A mother and a son live there. The room with the stuff in it is the son's room."

"Well, it tells me the son is around, but maybe the mother is gone, or has died."

"But nothing ever changes in the son's room," I said.

"For weeks?"

"For years. In fact, for decades."

"Same answer: I'd say the son is still alive. He's just not there at present. He's away. He's somewhere else."

"Okay, let's say the son is not alive either — that he died too."

"Then that makes it a little more complicated. Obviously someone is keeping the house that way. There is some presence of one kind or another that's keeping it that way."

I thought about it.

"And who would that presence be?" I asked.

"What you do is, Nick, you start eliminating all the people involved — all the suspects — one by one."

"We already did that — we eliminated everyone. Everyone who knows about it."

"All but one."

"Who's that?"

"You, Nick. You know about it."

He smiled a crooked smile. He stubbed out his cigarette in a glass ashtray and sat on the corner of his desk, looking at me.

"You're saying I'm the one doing it?"

He shrugged. "It's your puzzle, Nick."

I didn't say anything. I sat there thinking about it.

Narmer took a sip of coffee from his cup.

After a short pause, he said: "I've got a detective puzzle too. Something I've been meaning to ask you."

"Sure," I said.

"The other day you were in here, you paid me $30 — you know, to look for your friend."

"Yeah?"

"Well, I was sitting here passing the time, looking at the bills you gave me — a ten dollar bill and a twenty. The date on both of them said 1991. At first I thought they were funny money — that happened to me once, from a client. But I asked a friend who was a banker about them and he said they seemed real. So I just made a note to ask you about it."

Narmer was looking downward, at his fingernails. Then he shook another cigarette out of his pack and made an elaborate display of lighting it, blowing out smoke, shaking out the match.

There was silence for a long moment.

"Also, there's a few other things. See, in my business I'm used to looking at people — at their manner, at what they wear, and so on. Are their clothes new, or are they scuffed and worn out? Are their hands rough, like they've been doing heavy work? That sort of thing. The shoes you were wearing when you came in here looked odd to me. And the brand name on them — it's a company that doesn't exist."

I looked at him. And then I looked down at my shoes. I felt like one of these people you see in a Perry Mason case who has just been found out in front of the whole jury. The jig was up.

I said, finally: "I'll tell you what — I'll explain it — I'll explain the whole thing to you, but I can't right now. Let's get together one of these nights and have a few drinks. Then I'll tell you the answer. Is that fair enough? It's not funny money."

Narmer laughed. He stood up slowly from the corner of his desk. "Fair enough," he said.

"I'll call you," I said, and made for the front door. He was still standing there, staring after me as I left. I could see his reflection in the glass.

PART II

THE AGE OF AQUARIUS

Time it was,
And what a time it was,
It was...
A time of innocence,
A time of confidences.
Long ago... it must be...
I have a photograph.
        Preserve your memories;
They're all that's left you...
        — Simon and Garfunkel

8

"It's odd."

"What?"

"Phones don't make that sound anymore."

"What sound?"

"That ringing sound."

"What do they do?"

"They hum... kind of a fluttering, low-level hum."

"Really."

"Really."

Ida was wearing her bell-bottom jeans, the ones with embroidery on the sides, and an ivory-colored, waist-length Nehru jacket. Everyone was feeling rather Indian on this day — almost Hindu. You couldn't help it. It was a feeling that was in the air.

"Also, another thing I noticed — a small thing maybe — everybody has T-shirts with nothing written on them."

"What do you mean?" she said curiously, "What's on them in the future?"

I shrugged. "All kinds of stuff. Slogans, drawings, corporate logos, college colors, etc."

She continued to look at me, as if wondering if I had lost my mind.

"No... it's a small thing," I said. "But I just noticed it. I mean... you hardly ever see a T-shirt with *nothing* written on it..."

She gave me the look again.

"Nick," she said. "You've been here all along, okay? You didn't come from the future. Now knock it off."

"But I did."

"How did you get here?"

"Drove."

She gave me her best deadpan expression.

"You drove from the future to here."

"Okay, forget it," I said.

We went downtown later in the day.

We walked past a well-known record store near the end of State Street. We paused a moment and glanced in the front door.

"You still have record stores, I trust," Ida said in a facetious tone, as we continued on.

"Yes, we still have record stores," I told her, "But they don't sell records anymore."

"Oh, really," she said. "What do they sell, vacuum cleaners and hula hoops?"

"No, they sell tapes and CD's — little inventions which replaced records."

"Oh, of course, I might have guessed. Tapes like scotch tape?"

"No, tapes like reel-to-reel tapes, on cassette tapes—"

"What's a cassette tape?" she asked.

"Never mind."

"What's a CD?"

"CD's are little disks with music on them..."

"And the record needle goes around on the little disk..."

"No, the record needle does not go around on the little disk. I don't know how it works, but it doesn't involve a needle."

She had taken a red lollipop-type affair out of her pocket — she was sucking on it seductively, like a young Lolita, looking at me out of the corner of her eye. She was wearing a pair of bright blue hippie sunglasses — of the type popularized by John Lennon. She looked at me over the top of them. We were standing on the street corner.

"How about TV? she asked endearingly. "Do people still watch TV? Or isn't there such a thing anymore?"

"TV?" I said rather testily, "TV, Ida?"

"Yes," she said, holding onto the sucker, "Is there still such a thing as TV in this future of yours?"

"No," I said. "We have tiny spaceships which hover in the air in front of our eyes and keep us entertained 24 hours a day."

She tilted her head to the side, as if she couldn't tell if I was serious or not.

Finally I said: "What do you think, Ida?"

"I don't know," she said. "That's why I asked."

"Well, think about it. I'm from the 1990's," I said. "I'm not from the 31st Century."

"So you still have TV, is what you're saying..."

"Yes, of *course* there is still TV."

She took the sucker out of her mouth then, held it suspended in air, turned it this way and that and looked at it. "Well you don't have to get huffy about it," she said.

It was one morning a few days later that Ida found The List — the list I had made of things I wanted to do. I had emptied my pockets and left it laying on a bureau at the Hog

Farm.

"What's this?" she asked.

"It's a list of things I wanted to do when I came here..."

She looked at it, her eyes very amused. One of the last things on the list was, *See Led Zeppelin in concert.* She read it and laughed again.

"What's so funny?" I said to her.

She shook her head. She was truly mystified by it.

I explained: "Well, it sounded like a good idea at the time. I guess I couldn't think of reason number 10. Art made me do it — the list I mean."

"Who's Led Zeppelin?"

"Maybe I jumped the gun a little," I said. "Maybe the group hasn't even been formed yet."

A couple of days earlier I had jokingly advised her to buy Aerosmith and Led Zeppelin albums when they came out — that they would be worth money someday — a good investment. Also albums by The Who.

She came back later that same day with twelve albums by The Who.

"What's this?" I asked her.

"Who albums," she said. "You said they'd be valuable — that I should buy some."

"I didn't say buy fifteen goddamn albums."

"Yes you did."

"I most certainly did not."

"Well, maybe they go up in value."

"You bought them for $7.95," I said, "in thirty years they're going to be worth at least 11.95 each — and that's if you take care of them."

One afternoon, a couple days later, she asked:
"What's it like being old?"

I gave her an annoyed look.

"I meant... older. Old*er*. Sorry."

I looked up in the air for an answer. Took a deep breath. "What's it like being old..." I repeated. "Oh, not that great. It's more fun to be young."

"Really? Is it?"

"Well, of course. Sure. No contest."

"Why?"

"Why?" I said. "Why? Because you get to be more irresponsible. Because all the best stuff in life is front-loaded, as someone once said. After a certain amount of time, it's all a repeat."

"Really — that's interesting."

"Yeah."

"Well, I mean, what else — what's it like? I'm interested."

"What's it *like?*" I shrugged. "What's it like... I don't know... Let's see..." I thought a moment. "You end up being more responsible — gradually, by degrees... You don't want to, of course... But eventually they drag you, kicking and screaming, against your will, into the great Land of Adulthood." She looked at me prettily, putting her chin in her hands. I looked back at her, and shrugged. "And so... pretty soon you're just this disgustingly responsible older person, that's all."

She was listening intently, chin resting on her hand. She bit her lower lip and stared at me.

"So then what do you do when you're an adult?" she asked with amusement.

"What do you *do?* I don't know... you work. You work during the week, and on the weekends you go out to eat — at restaurants."

"Gee, it sounds wonderful. It sounds like my parents, what they do."

"Yeah," I said. "Exactly."

"What else?"

"About growing old?"

"Yeah."

"Why are you so interested in this?"

She shrugged. "I don't know. I just am."

"Okay, let's see..." I thought it over for a moment. Finally I said: "You have a little less energy... not a *lot* less, but some. It's noticeable. Your energy is not unlimited, like it used to be... Also, there's a few big shocks that come along... You lose friends, some move away, deaths, divorces, that kind of crap... All the stuff you thought only happened to other people. It starts to have an effect. "

A little while later old age wasn't fun anymore, as a subject, at least.

"I've figured out your problem, Nick," she said.

"Oh, what's that?"

"You're too uptight."

Ida was cajoling me, and pulling me — she had a hold of my right hand and was trying to drag me toward the door. We were at one of the main buildings at the Hog Farm — the one where everyone ate at a long wooden table. It was deserted except for us. "Your problem is—" she said, "—you act like you're 50 years old. That's your problem. Come on, we're going downtown. We're going to snap you out of it. It's a beautiful day."

"Where we going?"

"To a happening — a love-in."

"You mean we're going to have to get stoned again?" I said.

She looked irritated. "Well, why not?" she said.

"Well, we were stoned yesterday," I said.

She rolled her eyes with exasperation. "Nick, what is the matter with you?" she said. "Suddenly it's like you're rooted to the ground. God, if this is what the future does to people, count me out. Is everybody there like this?"

"Well yeah, they are..."

She forged on, elaborating her theory. "Boy, the future seems like a wonderful place," she said. She began listing things off on her fingers. "Nobody has any energy; nobody wants to go anywhere or do anything; smoking dope is out, having sex can kill you; you can't drink and drive... Jesus, when do you people have any fun?"

I thought it over. Maybe she was right.

We walked outside and got into Art's Plymouth Satellite and began driving in the direction of downtown Madison. Ida glanced around inside the car as I drove.

"Nice car," she remarked, impressed.

"It's not mine," I said. She began moving over to the driver's side, rubbing her hands all over me. Ida, all hands. Ida, the human octopus. Ida, who could unbutton buttons one-handed while her other hand worked on something else.

"Whose is it?" she asked, not caring, breathing heavily.

"It belongs to that guy named Art."

"Is he from the future too?" she giggled, putting her hand inside my shirt.

"I'm trying to drive, Ida," I said. She laughed youthfully. She was wearing a tie-dyed blouse and a long skirt. The skirt was all over the front seat.

"I can't shift with you like that," I pointed out, "You're in the way of the shift lever. And to answer your question, yeah, he is, as a matter of fact."

"When am I going to meet this guy Art?" she asked.

"I don't know," I said.

"Is he a barrel of fun too, like you?" she said mischievously.

I looked at her. "Actually, he's even less fun that I am."

"Far out," she said. Then, while running her hands through my hair: "Is he cute?"

"No," I said. "He's not cute."

It was a beautiful day, a glorious day — just the kind I remembered from a spring afternoon in the Sixties, the kind you wondered later if you had just imagined.

"They don't make days like this in the future," I said aloud, a little wistfully.

"God, I just can't *wait* to get there," she said. "It just sounds so terrific."

"I was speaking metaphorically," I said. "Poetically. I meant there aren't sunny days like there are in your youth. They just don't seem the same, somehow."

She sighed and rolled her eyes. Finally she said:

"In what way?"

"I don't know. You seem to feel things more... when you're young."

She gave me her annoyed look.

"I'm just thinking out loud," I said. "But it's true. A sunny day is *really* a sunny day when you're young. A sunset is really a sunset. You really feel it, somehow. A breeze off a lake, a dark autumn sky spitting snow on a November day... a rainy spring afternoon is really a long, rainy afternoon... Later on, I don't know, it doesn't seem to have as much punch... I used to sit on porches, Ida... I can remember sitting on porches with friends from college, watching sunsets that I've still been thinking about twenty-five years later. That just doesn't seem to happen once you get older. Seeing a sunset when you're older is like... I don't know, it's like watching it on TV."

She didn't say anything to that. She looked out the window. Then she said: "Great."

Yeah, it was all coming back. I remembered it now. The feeling. The weather. And the politics. The drug years had come before the anti-war years. In your memory you just thought of it all as 'The Past' — you lumped it all together in one long, endless blur. But now it was starting to separate out again into individual days and weeks. I could see there had been a kind of idyllic time which occurred before all the anti-war business really began in earnest. Aquarius dawned before Nixon dawned. A more playful, Peter Max and flowers-in-your-hair period came before the flowers-in-the-gun-barrel period. The Summer of Love occurred before the summer of My Lai. The past was unrolling now at its former speed, day by day — a slower, more deliberate speed. Did I say slow? — slow-motion was more like it, especially when you knew ahead of time how it all came out.

The traffic on the Madison beltline was relatively heavy, and I was looking around, alternately marveling at scenery not seen in years, and leaned forward, white-knuckling it through the mass of steel and chrome around me. Ida caught this.

"Jesus, will you relax, Nick?" she said. "I've never seen you so uptight."

"It's the car," I explained. "It's just so... I'm just not used to driving this... it's like driving a goddamn tank. Watch what happens when I step on the gas—" The car made a throaty growl and instantly lurched forward, burning rubber.

"Yeah, so?" Ida said, unimpressed.

"Well, I'm just not used to it," I said.

For a few minutes neither of us spoke. We listened to a classic collection of Sixties songs unreeling on the radio — only they weren't classics, they were new. They weren't "old-ies."

We drove along. Ida looked out the window at the traffic.

"In the future you still have cars, right?" Ida asked, quite innocently.

I signalled to turn left, looking over at her with growing exasperation. "What do you think, Ida?"

She shrugged. "I don't know. Honestly. Does that mean yes?"

"Of *course* we still have cars. I've told you that. How come every time this future thing comes up, people treat me like I'm from the year 3,041? The 1990's is not that far off, you know. Ninety percent of what's going on now is still going to be going on then. Try to keep that in mind."

"Well don't get so uptight," she said. "I'm just asking."
She looked out the window for a moment or two. Finally she
said: "Well, are cars... are they... any different? Are they really
streamlined or anything?"

"Not really," I said. "A little bit, maybe."

She didn't say anything to that. She seemed somehow
let down by this.

"They have air-bags," I offered, by way of consolation.

That cheered her up a little.

"What's that—" she said, "something you sit on?"

"No — it's something that blows up like a life raft just
before a crash and protects you."

Her eyes brightened. "Hey, cool idea," she said. Then
she added: "But how does it know you're going to have a crash?"

"Because you run into something," I said.

"But isn't it too late by then?"

I gave her an annoyed look. "Look, I don't know how
it works," I said. "It just does, okay?"

"Where's it come from?"

"Out of the steering wheel."

She laughed. "Out of the steering wheel. Cool."

There was a moment's pause.

"I bet there's a lot less traffic in the future," she said
finally.

"*Less* traffic?" I said. "Why would there be less traffic?"

"I don't know — because the roads are planned out
better."

I shook my head and tried to remain calm. "Madison is
a lot bigger," I said. "There's a lot more traffic — it's more like a
big city, especially at rush hour."

"Oh," she said.

We turned down Park Street and Ida hummed to radio music and occasionally glanced over at me.

"Why are you going so slow?" she said.

"Will you get off my back?" I said.

In the early afternoon we'd had a few beers and I was
getting a little cranky. I was also concerned about drinking

and driving. I was over-compensating by driving slower and Ida noticed this.

"I shouldn't have had those beers," I said.

This set Ida off.

"That's another thing," she said. "Why are you so paranoid about this drinking and driving thing? I've never seen anything like it—"

"I told you — there's a big crackdown on it in the future."

Ida rolled her eyes heavenward. That was it for her — the final straw. "Oh, Godddd..." she said and looked out the window.

There was a long pause.

"In the future they've got this thing called the Designated Driver," I said.

"What's that?" she asked.

"One guy stays sober, and he drives everybody else around when they're drinking."

She laughed out loud at that. It struck her really funny. She put her hand over her mouth to hold it in. "Whose idea was *that?*"

"I think it was the government's, actually," I said.

"Well, we've got a system here too," she said, "the one who isn't vomiting is the designated driver."

"I know," I said. "I'm familiar with the system here. I've been through it myself. Remember, I've lived through this age."

She smiled and looked over at me.

"I'm not a space alien, Ida," I said to her. "I'm not from the planet Zortan in the 9th Galaxy. I've done all the things you've done."

She gave me a soft little pat on the shoulder, looked into my eyes and said, endearingly: "I know."

As long as we were disagreeing on things, I brought up the subject of a girl having endless boyfriends, lovers by the score. That really did it.

"It's called *Free Love*, Nick," she said, suddenly angry,

"Haven't you ever heard of it? You used to believe in it once. God, you sound like my parents, you really do... Also, I'm getting kind of tired of this whole routine of yours. You analyze every single thing by a whole set of criteria nobody has ever heard of, you know?"

Her face grew briefly red, as it always did when she got mad. She stared out the passenger-side window and said nothing for several minutes.

"I'm sorry," I said at one point, but she didn't reply.

I looked over at Ida appraisingly. She looked out the window. Her hair was blowing in the breeze.

Ida was playing the role of a hippie, I thought — she talked like one, dressed like one — but that was not quite the whole picture. While it was true that she was a part-time student at the university, basically, Ida was a working-class girl. Underneath all the hippie regalia, that's what she was. And that was fine too. In fact, that was one of the things I liked about her. Ida had twice as much energy as most college girls. There was nothing casual or aloof about Ida. She was on fire most of the time — intense, passionate. I had especially never met anyone so aggressively physical. She couldn't keep her hands off you. At one point, going out for groceries the day before in one of the pickup trucks owned by the Hog Farm, she was unbuttoning her clothes — and my own — as we drove through mid-town Madison... ripping them off would actually be a better description. Ida had no qualms at all about such things. Trying to seduce someone in a moving vehicle was no problem. Driving down East Washington Avenue with her blouse off was also not a problem for her. It seemed as natural to her as the morning sunrise. All of this, of course, fell under the general heading of *hippie* behavior. But she wasn't really a hippie. For one thing, there were always parts of the hippie outfit that were slightly out of kilter with Ida. She never got it quite right. She had white socks on, for instance — the kind that roll down around your ankles. Not that it mattered, or anybody cared, of course, but it was things like that. Or you'd see her in a softball uniform, for instance. In 1969, true hippies didn't wear softball uniforms. But there she'd be anyway, sun-tanned, ruddy-faced, happy as a lark, the life of the party. That was the endearing part about Ida. It was things like that — there were always a couple things out of place, but she made up for it in other ways. She might be dressed wrong, but later on, after the party was over, Ida was the only one you remembered.

By the time we arrived in the downtown area the argument was forgotten and we parked in front of my old college rooming house — a place on Mendota Court down by the lake. It was a two-story house with a sagging porch and faded white paint. I was surprised at what a quiet, almost idyllic little back-street it was — just a pleasant, narrow little street with buildings close together and leafy trees and branches brushing close overhead as you walked along on the sidewalk. I was surprised to find that I hadn't imagined it — that it wasn't just in my memory, but was true in reality. I parked in my old parking spot, the one I always used, and Ida and I set off, hand in hand, in the direction of the University Commons in front of the library mall, where we encountered hundreds of students gathered on this golden spring day.

Seeing it, it was all coming back to me, the feeling I had then. I had not imagined it either.

This was the springtime of the Love Generation, and the overall scene looked like a large colored poster of someone's version of Paradise. Ida and I stood for a moment marveling at it and feeling the warm weather and enjoying the sun on our faces. All the people there seemed quite peaceful and serene. It looked like a multi-colored Renaissance Fair... it reminded me of that painting of the *Summer Afternoon on the Isle of Grand Jatte* — as tranquil and peaceful as that. Ida's face simply glowed, of course, seeing it. Utopia had finally arrived —

that's what her expression said. It had arrived, even if it only lasted this one day. I remembered it now, of course. I hadn't dreamed it or imagined it. There was an intermingling of peace, music, and harmony in the yellow afternoon.

The Commons was jammed with people — standing, sitting cross-legged, or lounging on the edge of the fountain with their feet in the water. Others were simply laying in the grass. Everyone was dressed in the clothing of the day: bell-bottom jeans, tie-dyed T-shirts, beads, headbands. There was long hair, and electric hair in huge afros; girls with wide, frizzy hair, and others with long, stringy hair and drowsy eyes, and people who were meditating, sitting in yoga positions with eyes closed, faces turned blissfully to the sun. There were people wearing granny glasses and African dashikis and still others with top hats and tails, one man on stilts, and another playing the flute. There was a certain segment who were going "back to the country" — a variation I had forgotten about — dressed in overalls and farm hats — and others who appeared to be romantics, dressed in Edwardian clothes and reading poetry; and of course, everyone everywhere was passing around joints. There were a lot of pets too — dogs, mostly, cavorting together in groups, and one organ-grinder monkey and his owner, both wearing matching red scarves.

Off to one side an impromptu softball game was in progress. Hippie ball-players were wearing shorts made from cut-off jeans, tie-dyed shirts, and they were playing quite earnestly, but with an imaginary ball, of course, running the bases barefoot, turning up sod on the soft, straw-colored spring ground.

There was no shortage of eccentrics on the library mall this day.

And there was a certain feeling in the air. It didn't feel like the long-dead past. It didn't feel 'historical' to me anymore. It felt current, and colorful... and it did seem like the dawning of something — the Age of Aquarius. You could feel the excitement of it — it was almost palpable. People seemed to be streaming in from every direction... It was the place to be —

the historical place to be — join in... Welcome...

I hadn't seen it in so many years. I watched as if mes-
merized, and was pleased to see that it about like I remembered.
Inhibitions were being discarded. 'Ego-trips' were being abandoned — that was the message. Be yourself. Who you really
are. Feel all the old snake-skins falling away as you adopt these
new principles instead. Peace and love aren't just words, but
the end-goal of Man — the goal which makes all the other goals
seem paltry in comparison. I could feel myself being seduced
into the logic of it again, felt myself being drawn into it... A
young woman with a headband with yellow suns drawn on it
was approaching now, reaching out, taking my hand, and guid-
ing me toward her — looking at me in an understanding way.
It was a blissful look which forgave all my past sins... Forget
your inhibitions, her expression said — feel the sun, come join
us!

It all seemed too simple, but there was no doubt about
its popularity on this day. There was a kind of love in the air
which permeated the place and hung in the air over the library
mall. It certainly looked like Utopia and universal understanding were right around the corner.

"Hey!" Ida said suddenly, by way of greeting, to a young
man who had come up to us. The man introduced himself,
extended his hand in greeting, his sleepy face displaying a secret smile. I watched as he and Ida gazed at each other.

"Beautiful-Ida," he said admiringly, making it one word,
looking her over. "How do you like the scene?" He gestured
lazily behind him. Ida smiled back.

The young man was dressed like a frontiersman — in a
kind of fringed leather jacket and matching buckskin pants.
His eyelids looked heavy — as if he was very stoned. Soon a girl
appeared at his side who was dressed like an Indian maiden,
with Day-Glo paint on her cheeks and forehead. She was wearing a long Indian-type dress and moccasins and her hair was in
long braids on either side of her head. She pulled the young
man away, both of them smiling distantly... All of this seemed
to happen in slow-motion, in a blur of hazy sunlight.

The young man seemed about to speak again but the girl had drawn him away and they were gone. Ida shielded her eyes from the sun as she watched them go.

We remained there for a short while after that with the people on the library mall. Most everyone appeared to know Ida. She stood for a time hugging several members of one group of people near the fountain in the sun, and I watched her. She looked every inch the Flower Child on this day — barefoot, holding her sandals in her hand, her long skirt shifting in the breeze as the sun gleamed dazzlingly off her blue wire-rimmed hippie sunglasses. How young they all looked, I thought. That was the part I couldn't get over. I never really thought of them as being young at the time, but they looked very young to me now. They were just kids.

9

The Sixties was a time of personalities, above all. It was strange how I'd forgotten that part of it. But yes, how they loved people, and personalities then. Even the small things — the cut of a friend's hair, the way it fell across his eye, his long Pancho Villa moustache or shoulder-length hair, or beard; his laugh, the quick smile... People mattered, I thought.

They were in opposition to what they called the anonymous bureaucrats, the faceless functionaries of government — so in retaliation, almost, these were the years of people. Of personalities. And who could forget some of them... The various smiling and painted faces of the counterculture — all with the strange names too: Cotton John, Zephyr, Rock Bottom, Sarge, Moondog, Chalky, Star... The people with the gentle souls and good hearts — the people dressed in odd combinations of clothes or a face painted like the American flag who linked arms — all of these people with the bright gleams in their eyes and youth...

It was extraordinary to see it again. No one looked *past* other people... That was what struck me. This was different than in later years, I thought, when other people tended to become more anonymous — more like faceless mannequins who were standing between us and our career-goals — not quite people really, simply figures we interacted with briefly before moving on to someone else... People were... *customers,* or they were *clients...* They never seemed to make it past that stage. Not quite people anyway — they were at that stage just before they turn into people, when the outlines haven't quite filled in yet. But the problem was no one ever made it past this stage; everyone stayed faces in a crowd. But now, though, people were real — definitely flesh and blood.

Also, there seemed to be great camaraderie. Condemnation by society was pretty universal, and this made for a certain bond. Outsiders could be spotted in a minute — insiders could be spotted even quicker. There was a silent form of communication which went on between them. There were people to whom you could communicate perfectly in an instant without even speaking — with a look, a wink, a knowing smile. There was also a strength in numbers — in knowing that on every street corner were compatriots who felt exactly as you did — ready to flash the peace sign or come to your aid, comrades everywhere who would link arms with you... Seeing this vast fellowship again was quite tempting, made you almost want to join it... Mainly, you wanted to join in the mood they were feeling... I felt a sudden, great fondness for them. They felt the sun — if nothing else, the weather, the moment — they felt the sun.

And of course all this was going on on a national level too. There were all these strong people — John Fogarty of Creedence Clearwater Revival and Stephen Stills and Dylan and Country Joe, John Lennon and Jim Morrison and Grace Slick, Joan Baez, Arlo Guthrie, George Harrison, Neil Young... All spread out across the country... A united front. The young nation which was rising up was ready to face any future with such people at the helm, their voices ringing out clearly on warm spring days...

There was an elemental power of youth in them and they were all — of course — uncompromising. That went without saying. They were the Thomas Paines and Thomas Jeffersons of America's New Age. They could carry an American flag over one shoulder and a fist thrust into the air. The idea of compromising was not considered. Principles were not compromised. It was a given — something so automatic it wasn't even discussed. There was no way that time could wear such people as these down. They were simply too strong and there were too many of them.

As Ida and I watched the activities on the Commons, the crowd seemed to grow in number, people coming from every direction. The mood was intoxicating — a musical and Renaissance Fair.

The Beatles' album, *Sgt. Pepper's Lonely Hearts Club Band* must have been playing on a local radio station because its sounds were coming out of radios all over the Commons, drifting above the crowd — familiar kaleidoscopic images of rocking horse people and marmalade skies floating on the spring air...

I had noticed the glow come over Ida's face when we first arrived at the library mall and now I felt the same glow come over my own. Ida observed this proudly. "Well, it's about time you're getting into the spirit," she said. I held onto her hand; she reached up and kissed me on the cheek lovingly.

For the longest time we stood there, as if time had stopped — we seemed unable to do anything except stare at the people, transfixed. It had the appearance of a slow-motion, choreographed ballet — each motion seemed very smooth, fluid, and full of harmony... It was an illusion, certainly. But when I compared it to certain aspects the 1990's, briefly, I was starting to get the feeling that I didn't care if I ever went back.

On the other side of the political ledger of course, in these years, was a darker side... It was also a world of hard-eyed politicians in smoke-filled rooms, talking tough in the shadows... The hippie strategy in these years, in order to counteract this — the strategy for the coming Revolution (the students were going to change the world) was simple: they were going to change the entire *mood* of the world. That was the way it was going to work. This would be achieved, not through subversive or revolutionary means, but in another way — *gently*: by simply marching over the line of the horizon with arms linked, everyone together in their health and innocence and idealism, wearing the ragtag colors of Sgt. Pepper's perhaps, Beatles haircuts, moustaches, wire-rimmed glasses. This was the foolproof approach; the unstoppable one. It was the quiet, flower-bedecked approach of the Maharishi. It was by this means that they would wrest control of the world from the shadowy Jimmy Hoffa types and Roy Cohn types and Richard Nixon types. That's how they would do it. It was by this means that they would defeat the dark politics of the smoke-filled rooms. They would do it simply — through innocence, by changing the *mood* of everything they touched — to the sun. They would do it above-board, gently — perhaps in the way that Christ worked, as a matter of fact — hands outstretched, a look of gentleness on one's face, a touch on the shoulder of the other person... And then, moving on to the next person, and the next... This was how it was going to work.

After we left the Commons, Ida and I walked up State Street to a small *head shop* which was located on a side street. It was run by a friend of Ida's. As we opened the door, the sound of a bell tinkled, and we were greeted with a thick aroma of incense hovering in the air of the small shop. Ida's friend was sitting behind the counter in an old wooden rocker with his feet up on a desk. He was wearing blue jeans, a tie-dyed T-shirt and a red neckerchief and he had his hair tied in back in a pony-tail. It seemed to dawn on him only very slowly that he knew Ida. "Ida, is that you?" he said drowsily, as if peering at us from a great distance. Then he broke into a smile, recognizing her. Everything in the little shop was quaint and warm and friendly, like the spring day itself. There was a bookshelf along one wall and light coming in through the window, dust particles floating in the sunbeams, rising up in a general miasma of soot, shadows and incense smoke.

I looked around carefully at the room. There were crudely printed pamphlets on how to grow marijuana, large decals with marijuana symbols on them and a rack of T-shirts with various slogans of the day; on a shelf there were packages of incense and "adult" comic books — Krumb comics, as they were called. Tapestries were hanging about on the walls and several smudged glass display cases contained rows of roach clips, hash pipes carved out of rounded wood, others of polished bone, and others still of shining brass pieces. Cigarette rolling papers of every flavor were arranged in rows, each with the picture of the little Zig Zag man on the front with the smile and the little goatee... The incense was coming from somewhere out of sight behind a curtain in a back room, and also, from an unseen stereo speaker somewhere, music was playing softly.

Ida purchased a shining brass incense-burner with a pointed top. It looked like the kind you rub to make a genie come out of. The man wrapped it carefully in tissue paper and put it in a box.

"He's a nice guy," she remarked as we were leaving,

"He's a poet, too."

On the way back down State Street, we passed the sandwich shop known as The Pad — I stood there and looked in the window, fascinated, seeing its jumble of chairs that I had remembered from many years ago, and the man standing behind the counter in the white apron... Ida had to pull me away. "They tear the place down..." I told her, "No wait, some other business goes in there..."

"I don't care," Ida said pointedly, "Come on. It takes forever to go anywhere with you. You have to stop every step on the way."

Farther along we encountered a group of Hare Krishna people in white robes and shaved heads, and beyond them, groups of Street People standing in an open storefront. The window of the store had a long crack in it which was covered by gray duct tape and there was a black spray-painted piece of graffiti referring to Che Gueverra along with a crude outline of a large black fist. The high-pitched lament of Janis Joplin was issuing from the open door and people were moving in and out of the store. I started to go in, fascinated, but Ida grabbed me again and pulled me on down the street. I marveled at the sight of it all on this warm, carefree day. State Street was just a street then, it had not yet been turned into a mall, and in every doorway lounged some happy, grinning member of the counter-culture, every one of them wearing bib overalls, colorful Hindu clothing or other mismatched items, all sitting on the stoops in the sun. They were everywhere — as far as the eye could see. It was amazing. There were such huge numbers of them... they seemed to have taken over the city.

Ida and I passed other familiar buildings as we walked down the street, finally stopping in front of Rennebohm's drugstore at the bottom of State street. I had a sudden urge to have a bowl of soup.

Ida suggested going back out to the Hog Farm.

"I meant now," I said. Then I asked:

"Are there microwaves yet?"

She looked at me, arched an eyebrow and said: "Excuse

me?"

"Are there microwaves yet?" I said again.

"I heard you the first time," she said. "What is that supposed to mean?"

"Microwaves — I guess that means they haven't been invented yet—"

She stood on the sidewalk and stared at me, searching my face with her eyes, as if trying to ascertain my real motivation for asking such a question.

I said: "Look — it's hard to remember when things are invented — you know, stuff just kind of... comes along, you don't pay attention to what year it was, or when it first..."

She continued to stare at me.

"Never mind," I said. "Let's go in the damn drugstore here and have a bowl of soup."

She was still standing there, staring at me.

I put my hand on her shoulder, leaned forward, looked her in the eyes, and said: "Let's go, dear."

Once inside, I was amazed by the ridiculously small price for soup on the menu — 30 cents or something like that. I couldn't believe how much things cost. Ida had a strawberry malt that cost 39 cents.

She saw me smiling to myself.

"What's so funny?" she asked.

"The prices. They're so ridiculous."

"In the future everything costs more?"

"Are you kidding?" I said. "Cars cost about $20,000. Major league baseball players make about $5 million a year. Things have gone up — definitely. You don't notice it until you're around here and you see how cheap everything is."

That got her attention. Her mouth dropped open.

"Wow..." she said.

"A pack of cigarettes costs about $25 dollars," I told her.

"Really?"

"No," I said, and laughed, "I was just kidding."

She hit me on the arm.

I was still seeing it as a place, rather than a time. It was like a geographical place I had traveled to — that's the way it felt. Like you were on vacation in some mythical Bora-Bora which, through government decree, still had 1950's prices. It didn't feel like the past at all. It was simply reality with all the malls missing.

We had the soup and the strawberry malt and finished them while we talked. This done, I began to pay and put some coins on the counter until, remembering Narmer, I caught myself and quickly drew them back. Ida looked at me in a puzzled way, and then we went outside and made our way up the street toward campus.

"What was that back there with the money?" she asked.

"Collector's items," I explained, "Money from the future — I'd just as soon not spend it. Might be valuable some-day."

I reached in my pocket and handed her a coin.

She looked at it in amazement. It was stamped 1989. I don't think until that moment that she really believed it was true.

At the corner in the distance I could see Chadbourne Hall — a great modern skyscraper — a dorm for young women, fourteen or fifteen stories high. My memory flashed back fondly to an earlier time in my life when I had brought a girl back there for the curfew. I remembered the great desk in the lobby and the matron sitting behind the desk, and I remembered all the college couples hovering around the doorway outside in the night just before curfew — fifteen or twenty couples standing around, all making the most of their last minutes together, all kissing like so many moths around the lights...

Seeing it brought back memories of other days I had forgotten. The beautiful spring days at Peter Hines' house, for instance — I had forgotten them completely. The bright spring sunshine of that year, and the way it always felt around

suppertime when the sun went down... That springtime —
there had been something wonderful about it... Long after-
noons sitting on Hines' wooden porch hearing the rain drip in
the early spring. And after supper, the streetlights at dusk,
feeling the cooling air...

Timeless days — sitting and reading books on Hines'
porch, the braaaaaack of motorcycles sounding for the first
time on the springtime streets... And the summer days, too,
later on in that year...

It reminded me that the Sixties weren't actually how
they are sometimes portrayed. There were hippies, of course,
but there were also real characters and real people at the time...
The *actual* people who were there, for the most part, were just
people — not stereotypes, as they later became in historical
memory. Your close friends, many of the people you knew...
There were people riding buses and people sitting in coffee
shops, and men driving street-sweepers in the dawn of early
mornings; people walking on their way to work... In some ways
it was less golden, less 'epochal' than it was written up to be
later. It was more ordinary. There were students wearing
sweatshirts and jeans playing poker in dorm rooms, freshmen
going through the enrollment process at the Red Gym, standing in line wearing their J.C. Penney's shirts and slacks... You
sometimes forgot that this was the Sixties too — that it wasn't
all California Love-ins and Be-ins, the way it was portrayed
later in Time-Life books...

I reflected on this, and for some reason it made me
think of Callahan — another friend from that time. Callahan,
who I hadn't thought of in years — originally a friend from the
freshman dorm, and his girlfriend, too — what was her name?
Debbie? I had to smile to myself, thinking about it. God, it was
all coming back... There was always one of them every year
from one of the wealthy areas of the state, and that had been
Callahan that year; his father was in brewing or something in
Milwaukee. I remembered all the rest of them now, too — the
whole group from the freshman dorm — Gerald Sterkowicz —
"Sterkie" and Cromartie, and Vincenty and Swanton.... All these

names suddenly came back to me... In my mind's eye I could see them all smiling out at me like a group photo — eager, adolescent — all different nationalities too, like in one of those old World War II movies: the Italian guy, the Jewish guy, the Irish guy; the English kid whose folks had recently moved to the states; the rosy-cheeked one from Iowa; the blond-haired surfer — the muscular ones and the slobs and the cry-babies and the lovers. It all came back — the great foreboding feeling of those first days in college, the heightened senses — a kind of fear that sharpened it: great striking dawns which came up — serious, sober — just not knowing what the future held at all... and that weak sun always coming up over the horizon, peeking up over the other freshman dorms...

I thought of all of them now — all the ones I hadn't thought of in years. Each dorm, of course, had one guy whose nickname was "Animal" — this was a guy who could tear the top off a beer can with his teeth, usually a guy with a muscular build, big arms and Cro-Magnon features... He usually dressed in frayed sweatshirts with the arms torn off; his personal hygiene was less than desirable, everyone made fun of him, and he loved every minute of it. God, whatever happened to these people... What became of them? There were the ones from the big cities too, out East somewhere — New York, Boston — young men who were impossibly worldly, who seemed like they were closer to 41 than 19. They knew everything, of course. They were going to run for Congress, maybe, when they got out... Or possibly take a job in a law firm making $60,000 a year, they hadn't quite decided yet...

And of course, to match up with all of them — it went without saying — were all the girlfriends. Debbie. Janice. Jo-Anne. Jane. All the girlfriends of all the boys of all the years.

All the ones who were *going steady*; all the ones with the fights and arguments always going on. Jo-Anne says we should get pinned. Carol and I broke up. Jane won't take the pill. Ann says we should spend more time apart, seeing other people.

And there was always one guy who was going with a

girl whose nickname was Starchild — something like that... some part of this new rising world that was coming into being — a young woman who appeared like a beatific apparition, who passed through the era like a ghost... And others too, of course, endless others — beautiful women drifting languorously through the era... Where did they all go? I wondered. Where did they all end up?

I reflected on this as we strolled along State Street on the cooling spring afternoon — I thought of them all, all the members of my freshman dorm, now all gone to adulthood...

10

T oward evening Ida and I were sitting on two bar stools in the "KK" — the Kollege Klub bar — a bar which years later would be torn down to put up the new university library. From my place at the bar I looked around and absorbed it hungrily, staring in amazement at a view I had not seen in many years. Also, surprisingly, I saw familiar faces — the faces of people whom I'd barely known, even then, but here they were again. Those people on the outskirts of your life, the bit players... now reassembled. There were the pennants on the walls from other colleges and the tables in back and the wooden racing skiff hanging from the ceiling — (members of "crew" came there, supposedly), and the little enclosed booths a step or two above on a small enclosed balcony. The song *Scotch and Soda* was playing on the jukebox just as it had been twenty-five years earlier. I was immersed in nostalgia, looking at it — I could hardly concentrate on what Ida was saying. I didn't see how I would ever be able to muster the will to leave this place — it was like reliving a dream. This was the bar where a friend of mine would approach me one afternoon and ask if I wanted to join him on a trip to LaCrosse, in western Wisconsin — a

trip on which I would meet my future wife, Diane. I could see
the spot where I was standing when he asked me. The outside
door was opening and banging with the long-dead but familiar
sound, and a handful of college students were filtering in and
out of the place in groups of twos and threes, some with books
under their arms. Ida and I had been sitting there for a half
hour or so, drinking beer, and Ida's cheeks were flushed, which
usually happened when she drank. She turned to me lazily.

"So, you're a photographer, Nick," she said.

"Yeah."

"What's that like?"

I shrugged. "It's okay."

"Just okay?"

"Yeah."

"Is it hard?"

"Hard? I wouldn't call it hard," I said.

Off to our right the ping, ping sound of a pinball game
was in progress — the old-fashioned, antique kind of pinball
game, the kind with the silver ball that bounced around on
flippers. There was also the smell of popcorn in the air. I
couldn't stop myself from looking around. There was a pleasant, collegiate darkness to the place. In my world this place had
been demolished decades ago.

"So you do weddings, that sort of thing?"

"The usual stuff," I listed them off on my fingers: "Weddings, reunions, graduations, babies, pets..."

"Babies?" she said. "Really?" The thought of that amused
her. "What's that like?"

"It's a nightmare," I said, without missing a beat. It was,
too — it was a nightmare.

She laughed. She took a sip of her beer, gave me a
wink, and said:

"I think it would be kind of fun."

"Fun?" I said. "Let me give you a free word of advice,
Ida — don't ever get into the baby photography business."

"Yeah?" with a raised eyebrow.

"Trust me."

"How about weddings?" she said.

I looked over at the pinball machine, at the young guy working the flippers and ringing the bells. The machine was of a year and model I hadn't seen in twenty years.

I said: "They're not too bad. It kind of kills your weekends, though."

She laughed. "I suppose. But at least you get a free meal out of it."

"If they ask. Sometimes they forget and you have to hang around the head table at the reception holding your camera and looking forlorn and hungry, until they get the message."

She smiled, and put her hand on mine.

"And if they still don't offer?"

"Then you tell them you're leaving — stepping out for a hamburger for three or four hours — that usually does the trick."

"But it's not hard."

"Not really. You see, in the 1990's they have these cameras that do it all for you — auto-focus, auto-exposure, auto-everything…"

"Oh, well, of course," she said. She threw up her hands. "What was I thinking?"

I added: "But also in the future the divorce rates are so high that you have to get the cash upfront."

"Well, I would have guessed that too…" she said matter-of-factly.

I watched as she took a sip of her beer.

"So how did you learn all this?" she asked.

I shrugged. "Photography? I just picked it up here and there — in the years after college.

"I never pictured you as a photographer."

"I never did either. It just happened."

I ordered us two more bottles of Schlitz from the bartender. For a few minutes, neither of us spoke.

Ida sat there looking straight ahead and I looked at her appraisingly. She was a striking beauty, but there was something else about her — the way she grew on you. Almost everyone I had ever known was attracted to her. "How's Ida?" was the first thing everyone would ask — and with genuine interest, too. "What's Ida doing?" was always the question of the day. You couldn't go anywhere without someone asking. It was a curious thing, really. You could look at her for the longest time trying to figure out what it was that attracted you and only then become aware of how long you had been looking at her. The nearest thing I can think to explain it is a quote I once read — something to the effect that "the difference between pretty girls and beautiful girls is that pretty girls are always pretty, but beautiful girls look different every time you see them." Ida was like that. She did look different every time you saw her — like a sculpture being slowly turned in the light. You found yourself glancing at her, then glancing again, and then a third time, until finally you couldn't keep your eyes off her. She saw me looking at her now and smiled.

"What?" she said.

"You're beautiful," I said.

"Yeah?"

"Yeah."

"Thanks. It's nice of you to mention it."

She kept looking at me — directly, as always. Then she smiled, put her chin on her hand and looked around the bar, slowly, as if pleased with my assessment. Her gaze came full circle and looked at me again.

I was still amazed by the fact that I was with her at all. This is someone who I was certain — one hundred percent and absolutely dead certain — that I would never see again in this lifetime... It was like hearing that a good friend of yours had died, learning to live with the fact and accept it, and then one day seeing them again. It was like that. And not just seeing them, but being able to reach out and put your hand on their shoulder... There was a kind of awe about it almost... And here, also, (if that wasn't bad enough) the same music was playing in the background, the very same songs I had listened to and associated with her for so many years afterwards, in my idle dreams, reveries and musings... And now here they were again, playing for real...

It was like returning to a fabulous dream you had once dreamed, and being allowed to walk through it a second time.

There were other things too: I found myself replaying the same emotions I had responded to her with back then, years ago — decades old emotions — as if they had been stored away in a vault and now been brought out again.... emotional responses I hadn't used for twenty-five years.

If anything, I was less intimidated by her this time around — whether from the fact that I was older and more experienced or that I was simply more objective about it. She had been a kind of dream for so long, one I had so embellished in my memory and imagination, that I would have guessed that it would have been more the other way — that I would have been totally speechless in her presence, but in fact it was the opposite. The years had increased my skills; time had *cured* me of her, in the sense that time always does. Also, a second element was: she was not a dream... she was flesh and blood, a human being. I could see that now. In the primeval state of youth she really had been a dream figure, someone on a pedestal, and I had subsequently missed all the blemishes. But now, older, I saw them, and her, as human.

Her reactions to me were the same, of course, as they were at the time — but I now saw those reactions differently, too. For one thing she was younger. She seemed more innocent, more naive, than I remembered her. And she seemed less sure of herself — probably because I was older and saw through the confident poses of youth. (In fact, everyone I met seemed less sure of themselves than I remembered at the time. There was a tentativeness about them that I hadn't noticed before, a certain amount of doubt which lay just beneath the surface. All I remembered at the time was the supreme confidence, the cockiness, the invincibility — and so it was, too, but as in all youth, there was also that slight flicker of hesitation and doubt behind the eyes, lurking just beneath the great poise and self-assurance.)

I also noticed one other emotion: an inner determination on my part to hold on to this, to grip onto it firmly and hold it very tight. A feeling that, since this miracle had somehow occurred, of not wanting to ever let it go again — not wanting it to end the same way as it had before, to just fizzle out and fade, the way all things do in time... To hold onto it very hard — even while, at the same time, I was not sure if I really I wanted to...

"What was 1984 like?" she said suddenly. Her eyes flashed.

I shrugged and said, somewhat suspiciously: "Why?"

"I don't know..." she said. "I guess... having read the book, I always wondered, you know. It always seemed so far-off, so futuristic..."

"It was a year like any other." I said. "It came and went..."

She seemed disappointed by this. It wasn't the answer she was looking for.

"Didn't anything happen?" she asked, "Anything amazing or unusual?"

I thought about it.

"Not really," I said finally. "Not that I can recall."

"Didn't they have a Big Brother, and dark futuristic prisons... and...?"

"Not to speak of—" I said. "Not any more than now."

"Who was President then?" she asked.

I was glancing around the bar, not paying attention, and I said: "I can't remember... Reagan, I think..."

"You can't remember?" she said, in mild disbelief.

"It was probably Reagan," I said.

"Boy, you're a lot of help," she said. "You claim to know stuff nobody else knows, but it's an effort for you to remember it..."

I turned back to her.

"Well, sometimes it is, you know?" I said. "Sometimes I feel like I'm on the quiz show 21, answering all these damn trivia questions about the future: 'For $5,000, who was Secretary of State in the Carter Administration?... For $10,000, who won the World Series, the Kentucky Derby, and the Stanley Cup in the year 1983?'"

"What's the quiz show *21*?" she asked brightly, "Is that some marvelous futuristic TV show?"

"No, it's a marvelous futuristic TV show from the 1950's," I said.

"I never watched it."

"Good," I said.

She looked around again, falling silent.

"Hungry?" I said to her finally.

"Yeah."

"Know what I'd like to do?"

"What?"

"Go up to Al Schiro's place — the Grotto restaurant — go downstairs, sit in the back room, and have a homemade pizza."

She laughed at this, then shook her head in an appealing way.

"You have the oddest way about you."

"What? I'm just remembering stuff," I said.

She sighed and said: "Okay, yeah, sure," and reached for her purse.

"One of those tomato-y Italian jobs," I said, remembering, "with a lot of sauce and the real tomatoes on the top..."

"And the light, flaky crust that melts in your mouth?" she inquired.

"And the Italian opera music in the background—"

"Let's go," she said. "I haven't had one in weeks."

"I haven't had one in decades. They sell the restaurant in the early 1980's."

"Oh, do they?" she said dryly.

She laughed then, and grabbed my hand, and led me out the door.

Outside on the street I stopped again, frozen in my tracks, and stared at the church across the street. Ida tugged on my hand, but I remained rooted to the ground. She was always tugging me away from some sight or another.

"What are you looking at?" she said, with irritation.

"That church," I said, pointing.

"What about it?" she said, disinterestedly.

I paused for a long moment, staring at it.

"I get married in it," I said finally.

She paused for a moment and shook her head and rolled her eyes in an exaggerated fashion. Then she pulled on my hand again.

"Let's go, c'mon," she said.

We walked on up the street.

"What did you say your wife's name was?" she asked.

"Diane."

"Where is she right now?"

The question stunned me. I hadn't thought about it.

"Well... she's... in town here," I said.

"Why don't you go see her?"

"It's 1969 — I haven't met her yet."

"Well, go meet her a couple years early."

"We're... separated."

"You're not separated if you haven't met yet," she said with undisputed logic.

We walked on in silence, up State Street the short distance toward the Grotto. I thought about it as we walked.

"There's a demonstration tomorrow," Ida said, as we made our way up the street, "Want to go?"

"A demonstration?"

"A demonstration — you know, on campus. Do you want to go?"

"Oh... Yeah, sure." I said.

11

I remembered the sound of glass breaking. I remembered the thinking at the time that no thirty seconds of college studies, no matter how brilliant, could compete with thirty seconds of current, real-time rioting which was taking place in the streets below your window. I remembered the way literature faded into dusty abstraction when rock throwing, tear gassings, and general chaos were going on. I remembered the way the hippies felt toward the *good students* — those conscientious souls who kept pursuing their studies nonetheless, making their way dutifully, slide-rules in hand, toward classrooms amid the chaos. The thought patterns were all coming back. All the campus radicals were dedicated to *input* in those years. Input was king. And if you stuffed cotton in your ears and went on your way to class and pretended not to hear or see, then you were cutting off part of the input. *Not* tuning out any input was the thing. That was the goal, the objective, the slogan.

The sound of windows breaking has a very startling and illegal sound to it. A time came, though, when you got used to it and finally you hardly noticed it. These were the thoughts that were in my mind as I looked out through the window, for it was going on right now in the streets below. Garbage cans were being rolled down the street; projectiles of one kind or another were moving through the air; bangs and clatters and shouts issued from unseen quarters...

It had started two days before in the student section of the Mifflin Street/Bassett Street area. The students there had scheduled a springtime block party — without a permit. Things had started out peacefully enough, but a short while later groups of students and police had clashed — traded shouts, insults, obscenities and finally smoke bombs, rocks, bottles, and tear gas.

Ida had been down there, of course. At one point police had gone into a house on Mifflin Street to turn off a loud record player and several people had tried to block their path — Ida among them — demanding to see search warrants before they searched the house. Relations between the police and students soon deteriorated. The fray continued sporadically into the night with hit and run vandalism, rubbish fires, and arrests in the downtown area.

Today was Day Three of this ongoing protest. There was a dreary predictability to it: a rally had been called. An Ad Hoc committee had been installed. A List Of Demands had been announced, mimeographed, handed out. The student body had been alerted.

The day dawned as a warm, overcast spring day and in the afternoon Ida and I joined a silent stream of students moving up the various side streets in the direction of the library mall. I looked carefully at the people around me. Students were wearing handkerchiefs around their necks, as if expecting to be tear-gassed; several were holding candles, and still others carried red flags, crude hand-lettered placards and banners. As the crowd moved, it grew in number, walking together on the sidewalks in silent waves, nobody talking much.

Ahead now in the distance, in the area of the library mall and the fountain, I could see the first beginnings of a minor skirmish in progress. A dull roar issued from that direction, a small crowd moving this way and that, shoving back and forth, with a dense knot of violence at its center. On the outskirts of this group there were other smaller groups, two or three deep, moving toward the center.

I could feel Ida's hand tighten in mine. We continued walking, skirted the activity on the library mall and moved with the main group of people in the direction of State Street, where we knew the larger assembly would be. When we turned the corner at the Kollege Klub tavern, a massive, chanting roar could be heard, rising up into the spring air. Our steps picked up speed almost unconsciously. As you got nearer to the center of things, I knew, the adrenalin began pumping, and your heart began to pound. As we turned the corner I could see the source of the sound: a crowd of several hundred was gathered along the sidewalks and in the street.

In my mind's eye, watching this, it recalled to me other days — events from a time which still lay ahead, in the future. A picture rose clearly before my mind of the grassy slope of Bascom Hall and long lines of police dressed in regulation blue, each with accompanying helmet and plexiglass visor and a long nightstick cradled at an angle in both hands. I remembered the statue of Abe Lincoln with small clusters of campus security alongside it, and behind them long, staggered lines of National Guard troops wearing their rumpled green uniforms, black boots and rubber gas masks, some of them from my hometown — friends, former high school classmates and acquaintances.

In memory the scene took on a quaint quality, a historical panorama frozen by the years — like one of those old paintings you see of the Revolutionary War — a tableau out of history. On the left side of the painting was the large mass of students and on the right were the troops, all neatly arrayed and outfitted, like the British troops at Lexington Green — Redcoats and Minutemen taking up their positions for a formal skirmish.

In the center of the painting small white puffs of smoke from tear gas canisters hung in the air — puffs of smoke as if placed by the painter at various distances in the composition, the white puffs standing out vividly against the pastoral green of the landscape. It was a frozen scene — frozen for decades in historical memory — but now it was starting to move... starting to come to life again. It had suddenly become freed from history, set in motion...

In my mind's eye I pictured several students detaching themselves from the scene and running forward, picking up tear gas canisters and throwing them back at the troops, trailing an arc of smoke through the sky. All of this in slow motion, of course — a blur — the trajectory of smoke from the canister suspended in the air like the vapor trail from a low-flying jet... All of it happening, too, amid the sharp fragrance of newly-cut grass of the spring, on some warm overcast day in some future month of May. Overhead in the scene, in a final element, a helicopter hovered and tilted crazily above the cloud of smoke, following the crowd...

But today was a different day — these were events of a

future still to come.

The sky had darkened now, and clouded over, as if threatening to rain. It had that overcast, leaden spring-feeling sensation that you only got in spring.

The protest march was going up State Street now, in the direction of the capitol, but at that moment, as we were watching, the crowd suddenly surged in our direction, like a giant wave. Swept up in it, Ida and I found ourselves moving with the crowd, pushed along involuntarily. When we stopped finally, we were several hundred yards farther up the street.

Seeing today's protestors, I could not help thinking of the way the clothing changed over the years. In the early days the students would show up for demonstrations wearing slacks, sports shirts and even an occasional shirt and tie. Later on, this changed to items such as black leather jackets, handkerchiefs around the neck, durable army surplus clothes, and even the occasional weapon.

Likewise, on the police side of things (as we stood watching, in the distance, a group of police talking together over walkie-talkies), in the early days the police showed up for the first demonstrations dressed neatly and conservatively — like policemen from the late 1950's. They wore the simple blue uniform and matching cap. By 1969, however, they had begun to look like NFL linemen and plexiglass robots who were planning an assault on Mars. Also, the vehicles changed. In 1967, it was standard police cruisers with lights flashing. A few years later, police cars roamed the streets with dents in the sides, windows broken out purposely and replaced by wire mesh, and even makeshift "cow-catchers" on the front for pushing through crowds. Beat-up looking buses with wire mesh windows began showing up as paddy wagons to cart away the rioters and arrestees. Yet the rioters became more sophisticated too, in their techniques. They broke into smaller groups, hit-and-ran, then reformed later. They used guerilla tactics. It was amazing how things evolved.

It was deadly serious. But at the same time there was also a play-like element to it. As the crowd moved down the street, from a nearby radio came the sounds of the song, *Daydream Believer* by the Monkees.

But I was reminded suddenly that it was not play-like, and not a painting, by my sharply beating heart, and the tightening grip of Ida's hand as a sudden crush of people once again turned without warning and almost ran us over, coming up the street toward us at full speed — many with handkerchiefs over their mouths now, others shouting, arms and fists waving in the air, and the crack and pop of tear gas canisters right behind them — a sound which was coming nearer, in fact, until finally, the sudden and overwhelming eyes-watering and stinging sensation of tear gas descended on us. Ida was a step ahead of me, running, pulling on my hand...

We kept running, it seemed, for a long time — what seemed like hours — until we were halfway up State Street. Finally, the sky darkened further and it began to rain lightly. Our sprint had carried us downtown, in the vicinity of Gilman street. Behind us I could hear shouts and the squawking of bullhorns in a kind of official-sounding, garbled way. We stopped finally under a little overhang of a rooming house to get out of the rain. Some of the marchers had continued on up the street, others had dispersed. People ran by us in small groups carrying rain-soaked banners and signs. Pamphlets disintegrated in puddles in the street. It was quite pleasant standing there — the rain was soft and gentle and spring-smelling. We stood under the overhang looking out, Ida shivering in my arms. As we stood there we watched one group of protesters trying to build a barricade in the middle of the street — looking over their shoulders for the police, building it hastily out of whatever was at hand: tree branches, trash barrels, pieces of wood, aluminum siding, old tires and finally an old mattress, carried heavily and comically into the street by two of them. One young man then tried to light this pile on fire — an impossibility in the light rain. The scene was completed when an elderly woman came rushing out of a nearby building brandishing an umbrella and shouting: "You bring that damn mattress back here!" She began hitting one of them with her umbrella and chasing them up the street. They all ran off, disappeared from sight as a group, and it was suddenly quiet again, with only the sound of the dripping rain.

I had ample time to reflect on all this as Ida and I were trapped. Trapped by the rain, and by police in all directions now. A police riot vehicle drove by, then noticed us standing in the doorway, apparently, and threw itself into reverse, and came in our direction. The spin of tires on wet pavement saw the car backing up crazily at a high rate of speed and we took off and ran out into the rain again, ducking our heads and breathing hard, down toward the campus area.

We ran until we were out of breath and by then we were down in the area by the University Bookstore, it's windows boarded up, and we took refuge in another doorway, when a similar police vehicle sped by us, searching for miscreants and malcontents. We stood for several moments leaning on the doorway, breathing hard, looking at each other.

"Nick," Ida said.

"Yeah I know, we've got to get out of here," I said.

The entire surrounding area now seemed to be controlled, in quasi-military fashion, cordoned-off by the police all the way up and down the street. The crowd had dispersed, gone who knows where, and the only ones left inside the area seemed to be us. If this was a battle, the police had definitely won. The landscape looked like a city under martial law in a

South American banana republic. At various points up and down the street, the police had set up small command posts of two or three men. The area was otherwise deserted — again, except for us — and eerily quiet.

Ida held onto my arm tightly; I could feel her shivering. "What are we going to do?" she asked. I peeked around the corner, wondering myself. The street was a no man's land except for the blue clumps of police with walkie-talkies, who were now wearing see-through rain gear.

We finally made a break for it, when we thought there was an opening, but the moment we turned the corner we must have been spotted, for one of the police vehicles wheeled around once again and took off after us.

12

We raced up the street and around the corner, jumped over bicycle racks and shrubbery, Ida grasping onto my hand, and finally up the steps and into the safety of a rooming house where I knew a friend of mine lived — Jack, his name was. This was a house on Lake Street — one which years later, I knew, would be a Hardee's — but now we ran inside the front door, slamming it behind us and breathed a sigh of relief. It was an old, ramshackle wood-frame affair used as student housing, which also contained, on the left side ground floor, a small record store called Lake Street Station. The front door did not stay closed when we slammed it — it was hanging from one hinge and we left it and galloped up the stairs to Jack's room. We pounded on the door and Jack opened it and we rushed in. He was wearing only a pair of blue jeans and had a towel hanging around his neck, as though we had caught him shaving. His mouth was open in surprise at seeing us, and he held a can of Gillette foamy in one hand.

"What the hell is going on out there?" he asked casually.

"A demonstration — which turned into a minor riot," I said.

"Yeah," Ida agreed, out of breath.

"You two look like you've seen a ghost."

We were still in the midst of catching our breath.

"If you don't mind my saying so," I said finally, "I think they're right behind us."

"Who is?" Jack asked.

"The cops!"

"The cops? What did you do, man?"

"Do? We didn't do anything. There was a goddamn riot going on, in case you haven't noticed. Look outside."

Jack went to the window and parted the drapes. He looked down for a moment or two at the street.

"You're right," he said. "It does look a little deserted out there. Also there's about three cop cars in front of the building."

I went over and stood beside him and looked out. "Let me see," I said.

The police were indeed gathered down below in the street. They were in the process of setting up some kind of tear gas launcher in front of the building, aiming it at the front door.

"You're about to be shelled, Jack," I said. "Where's the back way out?"

"The back way out?" Jack laughed, "That's a good one, Nick. There isn't one. We're on the second floor."

Ida was looking at me worriedly.

A loud bang was heard downstairs followed by several smaller pops. A moment or two later the smell of tear gas began seeping up the stairs and into the room.

"Oh, this is great," Jack said.

He didn't seem too perturbed, though. It was important to act casual about it all. As if it happened all the time.

He was still running the water in the sink now, rinsing off his shaver. He had a couple spots of shaving cream on his face and he had resumed shaving. "Certainly nice of you two to stop over. Drop by any time—"

Ida and I got some towels and a small rug and positioned them at the foot of the door and around the cracks to keep the tear gas out. It still seemed to be coming in, however. We couldn't keep it out. In a moment Jack had quit shaving and the three of us were coughing and our eyes were watering. The tear gas smell was starting to increase in the room.

"It's getting bad," I said, "but we'll have to wait them out. There's nothing else we can do."

Below on the first floor came the tremendous sound of crashing glass. Ida and I were sitting on the corner of the bed, and at the sound of it she jumped. Jack and I exchanged a glance.

"Jesus Christ, what was that?" Jack said.

"They're really working the place over," I said.

"They're going to come in here and kill us," Jack suggested.

"Nobody gets killed," I said.

"What?" Jack said.

"Nobody gets killed in this demonstration," I said. "So don't worry about it."

Jack looked at Ida. Ida shrugged and gave him a look. "Just believe him, Jack," she said.

There was nothing to do but wait them out. Eventually, of course, they would give up and go away. We were relatively safe —Jack had about four large locks on his door — unless they broke the door down, that is. There was a lull for a short time, and we all sat there, looking at each other. A couple more minutes passed. Sitting there, I realized they hadn't been introduced, and I said: "Jack — Ida. Ida — Jack."

"So nice to meet you," Jack said, and Ida held out her hand and smiled weakly at him.

I glanced around Jack's room. I got a little sentimental seeing it — all the various props, objects, and accoutrements of the era. These were the years, I remembered, of strange dark little apartments, hidden away — dark hallways and dim corridors. They were the years of sleeping on mattresses on floors behind heavily scarred, padlocked doors, far from the world, it seemed, very far; they were apartments upstairs — always upstairs it seemed — with endless dark passageways and rows of locked doors, and in the winter — I always remembered it as being in the winter somehow — the cold rooms, and no heat, and the people wearing their winter coats and the snowflakes falling softly and quietly outside dirty windows. The smell of incense of course, always, and the white clouds of opium smoke or marijuana rising up in endless eddies — rooms lit by dim red lanterns and candles and posters with black lights over them, but always cramped apartments that looked less like student apartments than opium dens of the Indian subcontinent. There were telephones on the floor and guitars standing in corners; there was sitar music winding its way through hallways and large American flags draped over windows. There were almost always members of the opposite sex present too, sitting there, or laying there, wearing only bed sheets perhaps, and looking up at you from mattresses on the floor with questioning and dreamy eyes. For some reason I always remembered this scene in the winter — people in long coats stamping their feet to get the snow off, and eager handshakes and scarves around necks, but here it was in the spring... What I had locked in as my recollection — the months of snow and cold — was simply a trick of memory... Jack's place was the Sixties, though, no question about it — it was the real Sixties: an intricate rabbit warren of rooms clandestinely interlocked together. The mood was somewhat like being a member of the resistance in an occupied country. But into this atmosphere there came at times wondrous people — friends who could brighten your day simply by showing up at your door, wearing the long coats and scarves of the Revolution, the inevitable guitar case slung over one shoulder and a three-day growth of beard, looking like Dylan. But that was in winter. The memory was always in winter.

We sat there for another half hour or so and still, below in the street — and somewhat surprisingly — they kept at it. I was surprised by the length of it, and the intensity. The rest of it, I wasn't too surprised. Hell, I could see their point of view. They had the heavy artillery, and by God this was their chance and they were going to make the most of it — blow a few hippies out of this one goddamn ramshackle hippie house, and have fun doing it. I couldn't blame them. It was what in a later era might be called a legitimate conservative viewpoint. But the expenditure of that much tear gas was a little puzzling. Didn't they have to account for that to the city council or somebody? If they didn't lay off soon there were going to be some red faces around the conference table when they sat down to review today's events — "We expended two hundred canisters, yessir, on this one house on Lake Street. Yes, it was a tactical mistake, sir." There was now this continuous, huge cloud of smoke rising in front of Jack's windows. They were definitely working overtime at it. The building was never going to be the same — it was going to take six months to air the damn place out.

"Why don't you open the door a crack," I suggested to Jack, "take a peek out — just to see what's happening—"

Jack shot me a glance, but then he undid the four locks and opened the door a crack. He slammed it quickly again. "Shit," he said, with feeling.

"Yeah," I said. "I think we're going to have to get out of here."

A little while later, with the cops still pounding away down in the street, Jack and Ida and I decided to make a run for it. The tear gas level in the room, even with the door locked and cracks plugged, was getting unbearable. Working together, we tied together every bed sheet and blanket in the place into a makeshift rope. The plan was to slide down out of the back hallway window. It wasn't a perfect plan, but it was all we had.

"We're not going to have a lot of tries at this," I said. "So we're going to have to get it right the first time."

We tested the knots and then, when there was a brief lull, we put handkerchiefs over our faces, ducked our heads, and sprinted for the back window above the stairway. The smoke of the tear gas was so thick in the hallway you could barely see ahead of you and the stinging sensation to the eyes had become almost unbearable. We held our breath, stuck close to the wall, feeling with our hands, and Jack quickly levered up the old window frame with a large screwdriver. This was not a graceful operation — it was more like panic, with a dose of the Marx Brothers thrown in — but the makeshift rope went out the window and Ida was the first one down, onto a narrow roof landing, then Jack, then I. In the rear of the house, strangely, when we reached the ground, there was no one around. We stopped for a moment and bent over just to breathe the air. I had never been so glad to breathe fresh air in my life. After catching our breath, we made our way up the block and then slowly circled around and went back down the street, out of curiosity, to see if they were still there. They were there, all right, still in clear view, still at it, lobbing them in through the front door. There was a pile of silver canisters near the curb, awaiting their turn. The group who were doing it obviously were a little out of control. It was like the commander was off on a break somewhere and the troops were operating on their own. Hell, I couldn't blame them — they were just getting a little practice time in. As far as the building went, however, all the occupants had long since fled, and the house was empty as far as I could see.

Jack and Ida and I made our way up Langdon Street then, past the fraternity houses.

"I bet the way they're going about this," Jack said solemnly, "There were a few people killed today."

"There weren't any people killed," I said again.

Jack picked up the tone of certainty and gave me a curious look.

Ida shook her head, muttering something angrily under her breath about "Giving the streets back to the people", and "Offing the Pigs..."

"Oh, don't take it so hard," I said. "They're just doing their job."

"What are you — a police apologist now too?"

I said nothing for a moment. She looked at me.

We walked on a few more steps.

"You have to root for the cops in the 1990's," I explained to her finally.

"And why is that?"

"Because there's more crime."

"More crime like what?" she said derisively, "Shoplifting and jaywalking?"

"No, more crime like serial killers, rapes, drive-by shootings, hostage-taking, and mass murderers..." I said. "So you end up rooting for the cops."

She didn't say anything — just looked at me.

"There's just a lot more bad guys," I explained, "Somebody goes on a rampage, shoots four people to death and it doesn't even make the front page of the newspaper anymore—."

Silence for a moment. She looked at me in a vexed, peevish way.

"I suppose you're pro-Viet Nam War now too."

I didn't say anything to that. There was another silence. She stopped walking, turned and looked at me.

"Always support the boys over there," I said finally.

"Why?"

"Just do it, okay?"

"Well, we do. It's not them we're against."

"Well, do it."

"God, you've turned into such a right-winger," she said.

I didn't say anything to that either.

We walked along.

Ida said finally: "You just don't know, Nick..."

"I don't know about what?" I said.

"About the cops. I was there, Nick — I was *there* on Mifflin Street the other day."

"There's two sides to every story," I remarked.

She wheeled around and faced me, hands on her hips.

"And what is that supposed to mean?"

"It means that the police are over-zealous, trampling on

"It means that the police are over-zealous, trampling on people's rights — and that's *one* version of the story."

"And the other version is...?" she said mockingly.

"And the other version is that the students are running around like a bunch of knotheads, asking for it."

That really got her.

"They're running around — as you put it — because they're trying to stop a war!"

I touched her shoulder gently, with my hand. "The war ended for me twenty-five years ago, honey," I said.

Jack looked at both of us like we were nuts during this conversation.

Jack and I knew this friend on upper Langdon Street who had a car and Jack said he'd see to it that Ida got a ride back with him to the Hog Farm. I decided to hole up in my old rooming house on Mendota Court till the day's rioting blew over. We walked up the street together and I kissed Ida goodbye. From a fraternity window somewhere the song *Hey, Jude* was playing — a long sad lament floating on the afternoon air. I embraced Ida; it was a reluctant hug — she was still a little angry at me.

At the top of Langdon Street we came upon a small auto tipped over on its side in front of one of the frat houses — an apparent casualty of the afternoon of violence. On the street next to the upturned car was what looked like a cop's billy club, broken in half. Jack picked it up and looked at it in wonder. Something about this evoked an immediate reaction in us — it became the symbol of something larger, though we weren't sure exactly what.

In those days, I remembered, everything was a symbol for something larger. A corporate lawyer tripping on a sidewalk was a symbol of something. A President wearing a suit and tie for a walk along the beach was a symbol of something larger. A middle-aged wage-earner with one glass eye fishing off a dam in Minneapolis was probably a symbol of something larger too. And this sight, of the car tipped over on its side in front of an American fraternity house and a broken police billy club laying next to it, clearly was the symbol of something larger — symptomatic of so many other things which were happening all across American society — but what it was wasn't exactly clear.

13

The rain had let up just enough to make the walk down to Mendota Court enjoyable, and then the sun came out weakly through the clouds. The street had a bronze-colored sheen to it in the afternoon light.

I waved goodbye to Jack and Ida and walked down the incline between buildings, finally, to the street on which I used to live. I approached the house tentatively, not knowing what I would find there, and climbed up the wooden front steps and peeked in the door. It was somewhat dreamlike, seeing it again, this legendary rooming house of my youth. Seeing it reminded me of the first day I had arrived there, suitcase in hand, many years ago — how large and adult it had seemed at the time — and I also remembered a couple years after that, the day I had moved out. It was funny how you remembered both days. This was really the place where "the Sixties" had happened for me, my major memory of it...

The first thing you noticed about the place, of course, was a certain odor as you came in the front door — a musty aroma of old wood, perhaps — also, the threadbare carpeting and the beat-up Coke machine standing in the corner by the landing, just as it had been on the day I first arrived. There was no one there now — that seemed odd. At least there was no one downstairs in the front room. They had seemingly vacated the house much as the occupants of Jack's house had on this day. I looked around, wondering where they all could be. I walked to the left side of the staircase and down a short corridor to a door I knew very well. I held up my fist to knock on it — hesitated for a moment, with my hand poised in the air. Finally, I knocked. "Coming," said a familiar voice inside, and after a short delay, the door opened. There was Alex, standing there, just as he had been almost three decades before. My reaction was worse than I expected. I felt dumbstruck, seeing him — I was speechless for a moment, even though I knew what to expect — for here, in the flesh, before me, was my best friend from college days. We had spent a lot of time together, Alex and I, learned a lot of the first things in life together, all those things you learn in college. We had fought a lot of the early battles together — all the little things that happen when you're coming of age. I felt a chill go up my spine. Alex looked at me oddly now, as I did him, and rather curiously, his head cocked to the side. He also looked very young to me.

"Nick?" he said.

"Alex," I said. I couldn't help it, seeing him I suddenly felt overwhelmed — I felt a catch in my throat, and my eyes started to mist over a little... It was... seeing him the way he was, back then. To cover myself, I looked past him, toward the apartment.

"Nick," he said casually, but with some concern, "I thought you were in Chicago." He glanced around behind me to see if I was alone. "Are you okay? Are you in trouble or something?"

"No," I said, waving him off. I brushed past him through the door. The sunlight was streaming hazily into the room, just as it always had been in those golden days of my memory. There were the posters on the wall — the one from the Beatles' *White Album*, another of Frank Zappa... There was Alex's long row of jazz and blues albums sitting on the floor just as it had been, his radio, the coffee table, the book rack, the colorful water-filled hookah pipe near the kitchen sink. Alex looked at me curiously — very curiously. There was a sense of peacefulness about it somehow, and calmness — as though there was no haste in the world — simply hours and hours of time — the sunlight coming through the window in a shaft, the dust motes floating in the light...

Alex said again: "I thought you were in Chicago, Nick..." Then he said, "Well, God, I mean, sit down — it's great to see you."

I slid out a chair in the small kitchenette of the apartment — trying to disguise it, trying to look casual, I let my eyes rove over the place, looking around hungrily, taking in every detail of a scene I had not seen in decades. Alex saw me doing this.

"What is it?" he said, with a smiling, puzzled look.

"Nothing," I said.

He had his hand stuck out and I was shaking it. He gestured toward the hookah with a conspiratorial look.

"No thanks, Alex," I said. "I... can't stay... I'm only here for a little while."

He watched me looking around the room, following my gaze with his own. "Really — are you okay, Nick?" he asked. "Are you stoned or... or in some kind of trouble?"

I waved him off. "Not at all, Alex, I'm fine, really — I just wanted to stop in and see you — it's just been so long, that's all... I'm just real glad to see you..."

He stared at me very curiously, his brows furrowed. Finally he said:

"Well, you said you were leaving — said you weren't coming back..." he smiled. "I'm just surprised to see you, that's all. I mean, I'm *glad* to see you, but you know..."

"Yeah, I know."

Alex was wearing his old torn blue jeans, the ones he always wore, and the faded blue work shirt, standard uniform of the Revolution. This had been pretty much the clothes everyone wore at the time. I saw him looking at my shoes.

"Nice shoes, man," he said facetiously, "Far out." I was still wearing the pair of modern-day athletic shoes, fashioned in bright fluorescent colors.

"Yeah, I..." I shrugged it off.

He was still looking down at them though, with perplexity, as if he couldn't quite put them with me.

"How's Brenda?" I asked. Brenda was his girlfriend — a warm, voluptuous girl who was passionately involved in the anti-war movement. I always thought of the two of them together. It was how I always remembered them.

The puzzled look returned to Alex's face.

"Brenda?" he said. "We broke up three months ago — you know that, Nick..."

"Oh, that's right," I said. "I always remembered the two of you as being together — that's my memory of you. That's the way memory works, I guess. It was always the two of you together — it's just a memory."

The curious look remained on Alex's face. He got up and stood at the window looking out.

"There was a riot going on out there a little while ago," he said, as if to change the subject. "You wouldn't have believed it."

"Yeah, I would," I said. "I was out there in it."

"It seems to have died down now."

"Everyone lost interest," I said.

Alex turned to me again, "Are you sure you're all right, Nick?" he asked again.

"Yeah, fine."

I continued looking around while Alex glanced down at the floor. "You know, we don't have a lot of secrets, Nick," he said finally, "I mean, if something's wrong, tell me what it is—"

It was true. The more I thought about it, the more true it became. He was my best friend, the one I shared everything with. The kind of friend you made inside jokes with about everyone else — all the rest of them — the whole rest of the world. It was hard to keep things from such a person. And now there was this kind of wall between us.

I shook my head again. "You wouldn't believe it, Alex," I said, "even if I told you."

"Try me," he said.

"No, it's too farfetched," I said. "I don't even believe it myself."

"Hey, we've been through a lot together," Alex reminded me, "A lot of weird stuff, as you may recall" — he laughed — "C'mon, I'm serious. Try me."

It was true. We'd been through it all together. Maybe Alex was right. If anybody would understand it, he would.

"Okay, Alex," I sighed and took a deep breath. I tried briefly to think if I was making a mistake again — as I had by telling it to Ida, and the Hog Farm people. I finally decided to try it, and tried to think of where to begin.

"What if I said I went ahead into the future and then came back twenty-five years?" I said. "Could you buy that?"

Well, as soon as it was out of my mouth I knew it was a mistake. You could share politics, or youth, or your first drinking experiences, or your first loves, or college, but there was a line, after all. I shouldn't have told him. Alex looked at me like I had just told him I had landed from Mars.

"Are you on acid or something, man?" he said. "If that's it, it's okay — just tell me. You can stay here if you want. Bunk down here till you ride it out."

I sat at the kitchen table for a moment and looked around and thought to myself. Finally I decided to try to backpedal my way out of it.

"Yeah," I said to him, "That's it. In fact, I did take some acid a while ago, now that you mention it." I rubbed my eyes and forehead with my hand.

Alex was still staring at me.

He got up. He went in the other room and put a jazz record on the turntable.

"Just listen to this," he said. "It'll take care of what ails you. Best medicine." He smiled. Then he said, "Shit, it must have been some pretty good acid."

He looked at me now with his old, faintly humorous smile.

"Wow, man..." he said. "You were in the future. Far out..."

He started laughing, and I laughed too.

It suddenly occurred to me what it must have sounded like.

"So what's it like there?" he said, still laughing his familiar laugh, one eyebrow arched facetiously. They all had the same reaction when I told them, I thought, I'll give them that.

"Actually, it's pretty conservative and boring," I said. I laughed with him.

"Yeah?"

"Yeah."

Alex slapped his hand on his leg with laughter. It was what I liked about him.

"I knew it!" he said. "Goddamn it, I knew it..."

We were suddenly back. We were together again. In synch... Sixtie's synch... It was just like the old days. It had taken us about five minutes to get it back.

He took a pack of cigarettes off the kitchen shelf and began to take off the wrapper.

"Say, incidentally — in the future, what do I become?" he asked. "I'm just curious, you know."

"A cop," I said.

"A cop!" I had never seen Alex so amused. "I become what — a cop?"

"Yeah."

We were both laughing hard by this point.

"Oh, shit," Alex said finally. He was wiping a tear from his eye.

He got up and went into the other room again, then came back and stood near the refrigerator.

"You want something to drink?" he asked, "A beer? A coke?"

"No," I said. "I'm fine."

He slid out a chair and sat there, rolling an unlit cigarette around in his fingers, still smiling. Shaking his head. "I become a cop," he repeated, "That's a good one. It must have been some good acid they sold you, Nick."

I watched as he took a cigarette out of the pack, tapped it on the table, and then tucked it behind his ear.

"By the way," he said. "There was somebody looking for you."

"Who was it — Art?"

I had called the hospital the day before and they told me that Art was no longer in his room.

"No, this was a tall guy, muscular, blond hair."

I thought about that for a moment. Some warning bell went off in the back of my mind, far back, I don't know why.

Alex got up, went to the window again and looked out. I watched him tap his fingers against the side of the window frame. Things seemed awfully quiet in the house. He appeared to be the only occupant of the building on this day. Otherwise, it was empty — eerily silent. Like any college rooming house, it was usually a storehouse of activity, commotion and shouted obscenities. Today it was quiet.

"Where is everybody?" I asked.

"They went to the Selective Service in Milwaukee," Alex said, "to lay down in front of the buses."

Oh yeah, I thought. I remembered it now. I remembered the day, in fact. They had all gone to Milwaukee to try to stop the buses from taking inductees to the induction center. Something like that. A couple of them even got arrested in the process. It was part of the organized student movement at the time — a couple of hundred people linked arms together and laid down in the street so the buses couldn't run. Yeah — that was it. The group was due back any minute now, Alex said.

I said again that I was looking for Art, just on the off-chance he had seen him.

"Now that you mention it, I did see Art," he said.

I was surprised by this.

"Yeah? Where?" I asked.

"Where? Right here," he said. "He's upstairs."

"He's upstairs?"

"Yeah."

I made an excuse to leave then and said goodbye quickly to Alex, went out the door and took the stairs two at a time to the second floor.

I walked across the carpeted hallway and knocked on the partially opened door of Art's room — the same room he had in college — and the door eased open. There he was, indeed, sitting up in bed with pillows propped up behind him. He was reading a book, holding it in his hands.

"Hey, Nick," he said cheerfully, matter-of-factly, "How's tricks? It's good to see you." He gave me a broad smile.

"Art," I said. "What the hell are you doing here? Did they release you from the hospital? Are you okay?"

"Release me? Hardly," he said. "I ran away."

"You ran away," I said.

"Yeah, I didn't agree with some of the medication they were giving me — some of it was wrong. But try to tell them that. Also, the cops were coming to visit me about that fight I got into, and so I didn't feel like hanging around trying to explain it—"

"So you came here," I said.

He shrugged. "Why not? The rent's all paid for," he laughed, "And by me..."

I laughed with him.

"Hiding out in your own room," I said. "Pretty cute."

"Yeah."

I looked around. The room was filled with books and clothes, just like in college days.

"So, how are you?" I asked him, "How are you feeling?"

"Not very good, really," he admitted, "I don't know what's wrong with me. I just don't seem to have any energy. I sleep all the time. Maybe it's just the after-effects of all that lousy medicine they gave me..."

"Yeah," I said. "Probably." I paused for a moment, then

said: "You know, ah... maybe we oughta consider getting out of here — you know, heading back. To where we came from, I mean — if you're not feeling too well."

His face was still white as a sheet, no different than it was in the hospital. He looked terrible.

He saw through this and laughed. "You're just worried about me dying and leaving you here," he said.

"Well, yeah," I said, "That's right. I am."

He thought it over for a moment. Finally he said:

"You're probably right. I don't like the way I'm starting to feel. Just let me rest up for a day or two and then we'll head out, okay?"

"Okay," I said. "A day or two."

Suddenly, down below, we heard a loud clamor, a lot of raucous noises, banging and shouts. The group had gotten back from the trip to Milwaukee. There would be about twelve of them, I knew — roughly the total occupancy of the rooming house. A cacophony of shouts, jokes, and collegiate insults filtered up the stairway. They were reliving the day's battle, each putting a different face on it. Laughter and one-upmanship could be heard in the various retellings.

I closed the door and talked to Art for another minute or so after that, before going down to meet them.

"Aren't they a bunch of morons?" Art said affectionately.

"Yeah," I said. "These kids today," and laughed.

"How's it going for you?" Art asked, "I mean, what do you think of it all?"

"I don't know... It's so... amazing, I just..."

"Yeah."

"It's... almost like seeing a former state of mind... like you're looking at an actual state of mind you once had, only in concrete form. Seeing it all laid out, just as it was..."

"Yeah," Art said. "It's something, ain't it?"

"Yeah."

I fell silent. It was beyond explaining. Art continued to look at me.

"Any regrets?" he said.

I considered for a moment.

"That I can't... *hold* it... I can't make it stop. It'll just keep going until it turns into the future..."

"Anything else?"

"I thought I would remember more... I really did. I mean, I've forgotten so much..."

"It fades, doesn't it?"

I nodded.

"It was all a thought—" I said. "That's all it ever was. You think because you lived it that made it permanent somehow — but it's not, it's all just shifting memories... It probably was then too, but you just didn't realize it at the time..."

Art smiled, sphinx-like, and nodded.

"There's also this schizophrenic thing—" I said, "like you're two people. Because you know your own future, and know what you ultimately become, you can see it all with your new eyes, and also with your old eyes... Very schizophrenic..."

"Yes."

I glanced around the room. Finally I said: "Well, I'm going to go down and see them." I turned to go.

"How's Ida?" he asked from the bed.

"Just as I remembered."

He smiled at this.

I said finally: "Anyway, I'll stick around, Art. Just let me know the moment you want to take off, okay?"

"Sure," Art said. Then he added: "It could be as early as a couple days — depending on how I'm feeling."

"Okay," I said.

I gave him the thumbs up and headed for the door.

He gave me the thumbs up in return and I went out and closed the door softly and descended the staircase.

It was late afternoon by now, about dusk, and already growing darker in the house. The hall lights were turned on.

As I came down the stairs, God, there they all were, just like an old photograph come to life...

"Nick!" a chorus of voices shouted. Adolescent voices, raucous, youthful.

They had only been back about ten minutes and already the aroma of marijuana was heavy in the air.

"I thought you were in Chicago—" someone shouted, a refrain I was getting tired of hearing.

"The Rube and the Geetch got arrested," Terry Garfield informed me.

"Hey, check out these tennis shoes, man — whooeee!" someone shouted, pointing at my shoes.

I took a seat among them on the old spring-busted sofa and heard the re-telling of the Milwaukee trip in several different variations. Terry Garfield was the hero in several versions of the story, blocking the police from carrying off two unwilling inductees, distracting them while they made their getaway.

The group was sitting in the *lounge* area of the rooming house — a small room in front with hundred-year-old wallpaper peeling on the walls and dull green paint chipping on the ceiling. It was a place of broken chairs, couches with springs and stuffing coming out, a single scarred coffee table etched with cigarette burns, and carpet so threadbare it was worn through to the flooring underneath. None of this seemed to bother any of the inhabitants, however. They were in their youth, I thought, it wasn't threadbare — it was colorful, distinctive. Next to the stairway, the mid-Fifties era Coke machine overlooked the whole scene — a rumpled and dented apparatus which looked as though it had been punched by generations of drunken revelers.

I sat on the stuffed couch and looked at them, without seeming to. It was a familiar scene: a large group of students seated at different angles of repose, all in the process of getting stoned and listening to an antiquated stereo speaker dangling from the wall. There was a hazy cloud of smoke making its way around the room, drifting in the airless atmosphere. A black and white TV set with a bent coat-hanger as a rabbit-ears was flickering in the corner showing *McHale's Navy* with the sound turned off.

Several people in the group were passing joints around, others were watching TV with riveted eyes, and two or three people were drinking Romilar cough syrup out of bottles. Scooter Malevy was standing up, announcing with great conviction, but in a rather slurred voice, that he was going to the Jefferson Airplane concert next week and he was going to bring Grace Slick back to the rooming house, where he planned on going to bed with her. Scooter was tall, blond and from Montana. This idea was greeted with loud derision from all corners of the room. Terry Garfield spit out a mouthful of cough syrup hearing this.

"Grace Slick is going to come back to this *dump?*" he said skeptically, "I doubt it."

In a stuffed chair nearby, Connor Thornton was reliving the activities of a recent trip to the Kentucky Derby with a friend from Sellery Hall. They had been to the Derby four years in a row and hadn't seen a horse yet.

One red-haired student named Beano was sitting in the corner smoking a large marijuana joint and reading the *Berkeley Barb.* In front of him on the coffee table were copies of the L.A. *Free Press* and the *East Village Other*, both rough-newsprint newspapers.

Another student was reading a *Sgt. Rock* comic book and drinking out of a bottle of Ripple.

A third, next to him, was playing with — and studying very intently — a small plastic magnifying glass that had come out of a Cracker Jacks box.

Roger Bowdish was slowly paging through a Classics comic book version of *David Copperfield* under a broken lamp in the corner. He had an upcoming literature exam, he explained, and the Cliff Notes were "too complicated."

Another discussion was underway about the best way to bail out The Rube and The Geetch. "Who's got any money?" Tom Sanders, the kid from Philadelphia was asking, and no one was speaking up or volunteering. A discussion then fol-

lowed about how the Rube and the Geetch, who were roommates, had bailed their dog Janis out of the dog pound one time
by sneaking in at night and throwing her over the chain link
fence. Laughter followed.

A song by John Mayall came out of the stereo speaker.

Gary Daggett was standing up explaining — in a rather
pompous fashion — that he was giving up drinking forever.
He strictly smoked "weed" from now on, he explained. He
revealed this lofty decision to the group in a condescending
tone. It was the new way, he informed them, the higher way.
He had seen the light and he had "evolved" onto a higher plane.
Gary was rather large in size and was attired in farmer's bib
overalls during this speech.

"Drinking is for yuks," he added, while a handful of
people around him, with cans of Budweiser in their hands,
glanced up at him.

"We understand there was a riot going on here while
we were away," Terry Garfield said to me, looking up from a
magazine, "Is that right, Nick?"

"That's right, T.G." I said, lapsing into his old nickname.

McHale's Navy ended and the *CBS Evening News* came
on TV. Several people crowded up close and began watching
it intently, looking for any mention of the University of Wisconsin or the Milwaukee induction center protest. The sound
was still turned off, however, and the stereo speaker played on.

One student named Santalla was sitting Indian-style
on the floor rolling joints out of cigarette papers. Everyone in
the room was passing around joints, starting at Santalla's end.

A Dr. Grabow pipe was also making its way around the
room with a chunk of hashish in it, the uppermost corner turning white with a tiny whisp of smoking coming off it, accompanied in its wake by a chorus of coughing. Incense rose up
from a chipped, well-used green figure of a Buddha sitting in
the corner of the room. The windows were fogged up and the
room was in near total darkness.

Santalla was still rolling the joints, which were laid out
in careful rows on the floor. He paused every so often to light

one and the twisted paper at the end flared up as he handed it off to Beano on his left. On Beano's left, Franklin Boyd and the young first-year student named Wiley were having a discussion concerning genealogy.

"Roy Boyd is your cousin?" Wiley was saying to him, with great surprise.

"Yes," Franklin Boyd answered him, "We're cousins. In fact, we're double cousins."

You could tell from Wiley's expression that this was going way over his head.

"We're double cousins," Franklin repeated, "That means his mother and my mother are sisters, and his father and my father are brothers."

I watched Wiley as he tried to comprehend this information through the perceptual fog emanating from a large-sized marijuana joint in his hand. He stared at Franklin Boyd. Then he stared some more. He just sat there staring, not speaking.

"God, that's far out, Frank..." he said finally, in a tone of awe. "No, I mean it, that really is far out."

Several other people were also listening to this discussion, and they were staring as Wiley had stared.

"Roy and I are double cousins," Franklin Boyd said again, with a kind of pride.

"Hey... uh... You know that guy... Roy..." Connor Thornton began explaining, very slowly and ponderously, "— Who lives next door... is double-cousins... ah, to Franklin here."

He said it so slowly that a peal of laughter rolled up from the group. Then Connor himself laughed — a kind of extended chuckle, intermixed with coughing and wheezing.

Gerald Karleigh, another student, came in the front door just then, banging it shut. He paused at the mailboxes next to the door and then entered the room with a copy of *Rolling Stone* magazine in his hand. *Rolling Stone* was an underground-type magazine in those days, folded in half on rough newsprint. It had been laying on the counter along with ten or fifteen copies of *Playboy* magazine which had been ordered under fictitious names. Above the counter the row of metal mailboxes was dented and heavily damaged, with the little doors torn off the hinges. Gerald was standing with the *Rolling Stone* under his arm, looking around.

Someone made a joke about the postal inspector coming the previous week, and then they all began calling out to Karleigh the story of the Milwaukee trip, and I excused myself and went down the hallway to Alex's room. There was no answer, the door was ajar, and Alex was gone. I made up a bed for myself on the floor. Nearby on the floor was the stereo, with the albums laying scattered about. Most of the albums were old and worn, and you could make out the circle of the record through the album cover in a white buffed outline. Others had names scribbled across the bottom in faded red magic marker, in the way that two college roommates use to separate each other's belongings.

I took out the record of *Sgt. Pepper* and put it on the turntable, laid the dust jacket down, lay back down on the floor and closed my eyes. I listened to the opening chords of the record — *Within You, Without You*— feeling them sweeping me once again across mystic time and cosmic shores... The lush serpentine coiling of sitar thoughts and images took me away to another land, a distant place, filled with harmony... I listened to it, and it occurred to me that a whole generation lived inside the opening bars of that song — in the space framed by those soothing Indian bars. I lay back and let my mind wander.

Life is a slow show, I thought to myself. Quite slow. That's what it was, really. That's the ultimate, final explanation. It's like walking through this long, endless bank vault in slow-motion — like Ali Babba, passing great treasure chests brimming with jewels — passing mountains of glittering diamonds and rubies, and stacks of money, yard by yard, and tempted always, of course — tempted by all that you were passing and knew you would never see or touch or experience — appalled really by the sight of all that was gone, and ever going by, going by... All that you were missing, always going by...

I lay there with my eyes closed and listened to the music and finally I opened my eyes again and looked idly at the woodwork on the window sill above me, at the wonderful carved detail of it. In those days they loved old wood, I remembered. Anything that was real, anything that was wood.

14

Day after day passed. The weeks went by. Art didn't leave. He was now doing research at the university library. He was feeling better and no longer spoke of leaving. I was with Ida so I didn't mind — each day blurred into the next. What Art was doing all this time in the library, I didn't know. It was what he did all the time anyway, no matter where he was, so I didn't think much of it. He never talked about it except to say, one time, with feeling: "Boy, do they need a computer bad." That was the only reference he ever made. His health seemed to have improved somewhat, though he still looked a little pale.

Anyway, now it was a night in June and Ida and I were lying together in her tent, her brown body intertwined with mine. I was lying exhausted, worn out and spent where she had seduced me. That was half an hour ago. We were lying there staring up at the ceiling of the tent. The sound of crickets blanketed the night — a long, unbroken trill.

She seemed awfully quiet, almost downcast, and had a frown on her face, so I asked her about it.

"It's my parents," she said finally.

"What's wrong with your parents?"

"Their generation — the way they've screwed up the world."

"Oh don't take it so seriously."

She looked at me with surprise.

"You're kidding," she said.

"Give 'em a break. They get old. They're not around forever."

I barely remembered hating my parents, and their generation. It was a stretch just to remember it. How much power they had — how invincible and solid and invulnerable they seemed'in their great autocratic hold on the world. And how powerless we were by contrast. It was hard to convince anyone who was younger to take the long view, though — to persuade them that the older generation wouldn't be around forever, that their power wasn't limitless, but was, in fact, quite illusory...

"Don't worry," I said. "Soon enough you get the 'power' — such as it is — and it isn't much."

"So just play along?" she said.

"That's right."

"But what about right now," she said angrily.

"Screw right now. Right now is nothing — it's fleeting. Believe me. That's what you don't know."

She fell silent, glaring at me.

"What?" I asked.

"I don't know... You just seem different... You seem so... detached, Nick," she said worriedly, "I mean, don't you get angry anymore? Politicians — Johnson, Nixon — don't even piss you off..."

"I guess not," I said.

She shook her head. She was disappointed — nothing could have been sadder to her than this.

"You used to be so..." she searched for a word "—I don't know, so vocal, so... passionate. You used to be outraged, like the rest of us. Now, it's like you're on valium or something—"

"It's hard to explain," I said. "You see, time passes, Ida.

Lyndon Johnson is dead. And Nixon is just another old guy in the 1990's — try to remember that. Soon he won't be around at all. It's like being mad at Calvin Coolidge. They're ghosts..."

She looked at me earnestly, trying to understand.

"Time passes," I said. "Everybody gets old. They get old. They become yesterday's news... It's like getting angry and riled up about the Spanish-American War. It's ancient history. And since I *know* that, Ida, it's hard to get too worked up about it."

"But... but the Viet Nam War, Nick..."

"It all comes in time, Ida."

"You sound like some kind of goddamn Chinese Buddha," she said.

"I suppose so — but isn't that the idea? Isn't that what it's all supposed to be about?"

She frowned. "I don't know," she said. "But I do know, we're *angry* here, Nick — angry."

"I know you are," I said. "But it all goes away in time, that's all I'm saying."

"Well that's just great," she said. "That's just fucking great."

She got up on one elbow and looked at me with annoyance, then collapsed back down again.

"I don't know what I'm going to do with you," she said.

Somewhere outside, among the chorus of crickets, I could hear distantly the driving beat of the song, *En El Gadda De Vida*, by the musical group Iron Butterfly. The endless drum solo was currently in progress. It was very distant, however, just a light tapping sound far away in the night.

There were also the first beginnings of a gentle thumping sound on the roof of the tent, the sound of raindrops on canvas.

"So when are you going back?" Ida said.

"There are some days I don't feel like going back," I said to her.

Ida got up and looked out. A moment or two went by in silence.

"Well," she said, regaining her cheerfulness, "It's raining — starting to come down pretty good." The thumping noise increased suddenly in volume against the canvas. She stuck her hand out through the opening, palm upward, to feel the rain, then stuck her face out, closing her eyes and smiling blissfully into it.

"Isn't it wonderful?" she said. "The rain? It's so gentle... so perfect..."

"Yeah," I said.

She drew another deep breath from outside the tent, keeping her eyes closed. The rain kept up. I looked at her.

"So what do you want to do next?" I asked her.

"Next...?" she said.

A familiar devilish look came into her eyes. She came over quickly and climbed on top of me, straddled me.

"Let's talk," she said. "How about that?"

"Oh, great," I said.

"You don't sound great."

"I'm tired of talk," I said.

"Let's talk anyway."

"Okay, let's talk. About what?"

"I'll pick the subject."

She held one finger to her lips, as if thinking.

"Tell me what it's like to get old," she said finally.

"Oh, God," I said. "I'm sick of the subject."

Her eyes flashed. She was strong and brown and young and she was wearing a string of Indian beads made of tiny white seashells around her neck that dangled down in front of her. The seashells made her seem even more naked, somehow, against her brown skin. Ida was almost totally uninhibited, I thought, which was either an admirable, or a not-so-admirable trait, depending on your point of view. Right now it was an admirable one.

"You want to hear what it's like to get old?" I asked. "Again?"

"Yeah."

"Didn't we go through this one other time?"

"I don't know," she said, and giggled.

"Well, I'm not that old, remember," I said.

She moved from side to side, mischievously, and her breasts moved with her, above me. She smiled at the effect it was having on me.

"You really want to hear this?" I said.

"Sure."

They were all very self-involved in those days, I thought. I could see it now. They saw themselves historically — saw themselves at the barricades... Always viewing themselves in some situation or another... They saw the best in themselves, though, and tried to move toward it... Yet the march of history looks down upon even such shenanigans as this, I thought — it keeps moving anyway, with its wry, mysterious smile. These things too, it would say, will pass. Even honor, uprightness and rectitude were a passing phase, something history smiles at.

It was funny. It was almost as though they believed that if they lived certain things intensely enough, that time wouldn't pass. Or, if they made jokes about it — with great facetiousness and wit and sarcasm... But humor and irony couldn't stave off real life. Not the best jokes, not the greatest in-jokes, the most biting of commentary. Time would still pass. Despite the sharpest of irony and humor, time moved on. The whole thing, witty or not, slipped silently into the past.

There wasn't one of them, I thought, who ever really thought that the Sixties would end. There wasn't one of them who realized that time was going to pass and the Seventies would come; and the Eighties and the Nineties... No, this thought never occurred to anyone at the time. Life would stop in the Sixties — it would stop there forever. A little common sense would have told anyone that this was unrealistic. But no, it would always be a spring day in 1969. It would always be a day when you sat on a porch with a cup of coffee, breathing in spring air, waiting for good friends to come over. Not a one of them ever considered for a single moment the possibility that, under the surface, time was silently moving.

"Getting old," I said to her, answering her question,

"Hmm, let's see, how to describe it..."

She watched me eagerly, reverently, her lips parted, hanging on my every word.

"I don't know... it's hard to describe... By the time you get there, it's hard to remember how you originally felt... It's like going from A to B and by the time you've gotten to B, you can't describe it in A's terms anymore..."

"Fine," she said, with annoyance, "It's hard. Describe it anyway."

I sighed, seeing her frown.

"Okay, well, it's like... you know, people you see around you who are older, who are middle-aged? That's what it's like. It's no big mystery. That's you. And your friends too — they get married and settle down and have families... they're no longer wild and crazy and reckless like they once were. People gain weight; get fatter, stockier... It sounds dopey, but that's the way it is. Your hair turns gray... guys who are your age get bald... that sort of thing."

"That's not what I mean."

"Yeah, but it is... that's exactly what it is. You just don't believe it can happen to you, that's all..."

"I mean, what does it feel like?"

"It doesn't feel like *anything*. You've got a little less energy, but having less energy doesn't *feel*... I don't know... Okay, let's say a friend of yours wants to go out drinking until 3 a.m. and you decide you're just not up for it. You don't automatically jump up and say, 'Great, let's go,' like you used to. Somebody wants to go dancing at four different nightclubs and you think, 'Shit, I can't do that...' That's all. You have six or seven beers and it takes you two days to recover.... You help somebody push a car out of a ditch, your back aches for three days. That sort of thing. Miscellaneous stuff..."

She didn't say anything. I went on:

"You slow up a little, start to pace yourself more... You don't think in terms of *topping* yourself and all your past events and experiences every time out... You tone down your act — the adventures, the carousing... There's less confidence that you're going to live forever and that your health will automatically bounce back no matter what you do to it. Is this making any sense?"

She nodded her head, but frowned.

"What are the warning signs?" she asked, "What should I be on the lookout for?"

"Oh, it sneaks up on you."

"Yeah?"

"Oh yeah, it's very sneaky," I said. "You won't see it coming. One day it just happens. One day, you wake up and there's this older person staring back at you in the mirror — a more wrinkled face, tired eyes, that sort of thing. One day, you notice that in your photographs you look like you haven't had a good night's sleep. Or there's this jowl under your chin, or pouches under your eyes. Every point where your body bends, you seem to have these wrinkles — deep, permanent, like used luggage."

She looked at me. "Great."

I shrugged. "Hey, you asked. All the older people around you — the ones you see now who are ten years older than you, or twenty years older? Suddenly that's you. That's who you turn into, Ida. Really..."

"It must be a shock... when it happens."

"Well, of course it is. Especially since, all you've ever known in your life, up to that point, is being young. I mean, it's who you *are*. In a sense, it's your identity... You're young. Period. And then one day, you're not. It feels like a kind of betrayal, in a way. For so long, time doesn't seem to be moving. It's just... stationary. And then one day you discover that it's been moving all along."

She was rapt with attention.

"What else?" she said eagerly, "How else will I know when it happens?"

"Little things. Actors on TV look younger; people on magazine covers look younger... One day cops riding by in squad cars look young to you, like they ought to be in college. And college kids seem like they should be in high school. And you see young couples... young mothers pushing baby carriages, they seem awfully young too. And all the people in bars are suddenly younger than you. As you get older, naturally everybody else looks younger. New fads seem... rather stupid. Younger people are doing them, but it's not your style. And their music is ridiculous..."

"I've felt that already..." she said. Her eyes were alive; interested, fascinated.

"I don't think you have to worry about any of this for a while yet," I said.

I pulled her down to me and kissed her. She made it a long, lingering kiss.

Finally she said: "What else?"

"You still want to hear more of this?"

"Yeah."

It was ironic, in a way. Remembering back, they never did like being young, this generation. They had always thought of themselves at the time, as possessing wisdom — and I remembered how they hated it when their ideas were dismissed out of hand because of their *youth*. How they wished to have these leathery, world-weary faces that would make people instantly sit up and take them seriously. And the irony was, in time your wish was granted. You got all the wrinkles you ever desired... You became as old-looking as you ever wished to be. That was one thing that life delivered on.

"What else?"

"Do you have any idea how boring this is for me?" I said.

"Oh, come on, what else?"

"Do you know you're very tanned?" I said. "You must lay out in the sun a lot—" I reached my hands up and put them on her breasts and squeezed gently. She smiled down at me merrily.

"Come on—" she said. "What else?"

"What else what?" I said.

"What else happens when you get older?"

"I've told you all the stuff I can think of."

She frowned.

"Okay, let's see..." I said.

I pretended to be thinking.

"You become ordinary," I said finally, "You don't mean to, but it just happens."

That was another thing they hated. Ordinariness. They didn't want to become ordinary. They didn't want to turn into typical people living in typical houses and working at typical jobs. And there was nothing casual or half-hearted about it either, it was visceral — they were *angry* with ordinariness. No, their days would be unique — they would pile up experiences, collect them. Yet a time came, eventually, when they were no longer unique — they were just average days. It happened like so many waves rushing into shore one after another — waves which eventually wore you down, as a rock is worn smooth in time by wave after wave.

"It's all genes, Ida. You turn into your parents. You really do. You get to be about 40 or 45 and you live in a house with one or two kids and you live a normal life. You live in one house in a row of houses. It's just the way it works. You don't turn into Joan of Arc or James Joyce. You don't turn into Mary Shelley or James Dean or Jack Kerouac. Someone does, but it isn't you."

"So that's what we have to look forward to?"

"It's all subjective," I said. "I don't know — it's probably not as bad as I've made it out. I'm just trying to explain... the way it seems to me."

"I hope you don't mind my saying it but.... once, you had so much energy, Nick," she said. "You were so... I don't know..."

"I've still got a lot of energy," I said. "I don't mean to make it sound like that... In some ways it's hard to explain..."

She didn't say anything, just kept looking with those bright earnest, youthful eyes, waiting. "I guess I don't understand."

I tried to think of another way to explain it.

I said finally:

"Let's say you were skiing down a long ski hill in Switzerland with someone — a guy. It's just the two of you, okay? It's a pleasant, crisp winter day and you're skiing down this hill. Halfway down the hill you're tired and so you stop and knock on this chalet door. It's a large oak door and it's answered by a balding, middle-aged man and his cheerful, pleasant wife. That's terrific. It's wonderful. You meet them. They both have pleasant, ruddy faces, and nice personalities. They are very happy to see you. They invite you in, offer you food and drink and a place by the fire. You have a nice chat, and you really can't remember having a better time than this and it is a wonderful thing to have such people as this in the world. Okay. But here's the thing — you can relate to this, but you can't relate to a world in which you *are* the balding middle-aged man and his wife. Do you see what I mean, Ida? But this is the way things really happen. The golden storybook does not include this scene. This is college, Ida. It's college thinking. I don't mean to rain on your parade, but these other people, right now they're like a backdrop to you... they're like a stage set... But they're actually real, and they are eventually who you turn into."

She looked at me, saying nothing.

I said: "You want to live in a world *with* these people. You admire them greatly — you like them, you respect them. But you don't want to *be* them. Do you see what I mean?"

She was looking thoughtful, thinking it over.

"I'm not an expert on this stuff," I said. "What do I know? It's just the way it seems to me. You asked."

All this time Ida had been sitting on top of me, listening curiously. Sometimes she had her hands on her hips, other times she held them down on my shoulders. Now suddenly she had heard enough, and she climbed off quickly and took my hand and tried to pull me up. "What are you doing?" I asked.

"I've heard enough about old age, now it's my turn."

"Your turn?"

"It's youth's turn."

She looked around and put her finger to her lips to indicate silence, then stuck her head out the tent flap opening, and looked around some more. Then she drew me toward the opening. I said: "Where are we going? Ida, I don't have any clothes on—" Still she pulled, cheerfully and insistently, and I grabbed a blanket which was laying nearby and wrapped it around my waist and followed her out of the tent. It was still raining, coming down pretty hard, and it was dark as pitch. I couldn't see where I was going. "What are you doing?" I asked again, looking ahead at her. She was still pulling me in one direction, as if with a certain purpose. She finally explained, in a loud whisper, "I've got an idea—"

"What?"

"I want us to make love in the rain."

"You want us to—"

She pulled at me urgently again.

"Come on," she said.

"Oh, great," I said.

Her naked form ran in front of me, pulling me along, a dark shadow, slick and shiny from the rain, gleaming in the weak light. I could hear the sound of the rain hitting leaves on the ground and felt them underneath my bare feet as I ran along — wet leaves and old straw of some kind, and after that a patch of dirt, now turning to soft mud. Ida was drawing me to an area behind the compound with many trees. It was raining harder now — really coming down. The area behind the compound was like a little forest, with a little stand of trees about a hundred feet square, and the trees maybe ten feet apart. It was dark there away from the lights of the camp. "Where exactly did you have in mind?" I said. "Just down here in the mud, or what—?" But she only laughed and did not reply, and pulled me on. She pulled me up to one of the trees, then she spun around abruptly, her hair hanging down wetly on the sides of her head. She embraced me quickly, muscularly — pulled me to her. "Ummm," she said, and laughed gaily. She said it again, hungrily, and closed her eyes and pulled me to her very hard. Her long hair, normally dry and wind-blown, was now in a straggled mass on either side of her head, and hung wetly down on her shoulders. Rain was on her face and in her eyes and she blinked to keep it out. She held my face in both hands and kissed me, her body urging me on.

"Are you sure there's no one else around?" I whispered, glancing about worriedly.

"Shhhh, this is youth's turn," she said again.

"Oh yeah, that's right," I said. "I forgot. And what does youth have in mind?"

"We're free, Nick," she proclaimed, "That's what. There's no one else around. We can do anything we want... We're like children, see...? That's what youth says."

She had her arms about my neck and she looked into my eyes and laughed again. I felt her body, the length of it, slick with the rain. She leaned back against the tree and pulled me closer to her, her eyes closed. "Right here, Nick," she said. "Right now, right here..."

She rested backwards on the tree, her eyes closed, dreamily, as if in paradise. The bark of the tree seemed deeply furrowed and rough, and I said to her, "Are you all right?" and she answered, "I don't care, Nick. It doesn't matter."

There was a flash of lightning then, followed by thunder and the whole landscape went blinding white for a split-second — but again Ida just laughed. She didn't even open her eyes — just laughed with them closed as if she didn't care. She was in a blissful state.

"We're not supposed to be standing under a tree during a goddamn lightning storm," I said, but I could tell I was wasting my breath.

"What a way to go, Nick," she said. "Think of it — wouldn't it be great..."

"Yeah," I said.

The lightning flashed again, with further accompanying thunder. It didn't sound very far off, either.

I started to say something but she interrupted me.

"I don't care," she said. "I don't care—" We were embracing one another and I felt the slipperiness of her skin with my fingertips and then she slid out of my grasp and a moment later we were tumbling through space and then we were on the ground near the tree, among the leaves I had felt before, in the soft straw and the mud. There was something very primitive and animalistic about Ida, I decided, something quite fierce and pagan.

We drove into town the next night and attended an anti-war symposium at the Memorial Union on campus. There were workshops on subjects such as non-violent resistance at sit-ins, the position of the University with regard to defense contracts, and so on, and later on in the main auditorium speeches were scheduled concerning the Movement's strategies for the coming school year. One of the main speakers was Erich Mann — someone else I had forgotten about until now — probably never thought of once in all the intervening years — yet seeing him now triggered my memory. I remembered him giving a speech on campus, standing on the speaker's platform next to Paul Soglin and other student leaders — Erich Mann, I thought, head of the original Clean Gene McCarthy movement on campus, the fair-haired boy of the New Left — I could see him still, in my mind's eye, fist in the air, green army surplus coat and blond hair blowing around rebelliously in a stiff wind, amid the rising chants of the crowd... I remembered wondering how a person rose to such an exalted position in the peace movement as this — Eric Mann, pursued by droves of young college women, a mover of men, a shaker (of fists), a guardian of the public good... How did one rise so quickly in such a disorganized Movement? What was the secret? The rest of us were simply the 'foot soldiers' of the Movement — members who made up the crowd — the student proletariat, the proverbial faceless masses. But how did you move up? On what invisible rungs of the ladder did you ascend to such great heights? So many must have stared with secret envy from the distance of the crowd — wanting to participate in this defining moment of their age — yet finding themselves only a member of the audience. So many others must have wanted to stand at the microphone too, with their fist upraised, inciting people to calls to conscience, calls to action... So many others would have liked to have had their hair blown by the wind, the collar of their khaki army jacket drawn close, flapping occasionally on wind-whipped autumn days — to have seen the history-making days from the viewpoint of the high wooden platform instead of the flat unending plane of the audience... I remembered all this now as I stood with Ida watching him again in the distance on the stage. I was probably the only one in the audience watching with amusement, awe and nostalgia.

   After Erich Mann there were a handful of other speakers and then part way through the program, to my great and everlasting amusement, the rally was 'invaded' by a contingent of Weathermen, a violent splinter group from some larger city like Milwaukee or Chicago. They were all wearing combat-type uniforms and armbands. They took control of the stage, threw speakers off who were waiting to speak, took over the microphone, and began giving harsh political pronouncements to the crowd— "the pampered sons and daughters of the middle class" as they called them, berating them unmercifully. The earnestness and pretentiousness of it were hilarious. Nobody else was laughing though. To everybody else it was serious business. Cries of "adventurists!" issued from the crowd — the ultimate put-down, apparently, judging by the tone and popularity of the chant. "Adventurists!" the call swept the auditorium. In a final melodramatic touch, a handful of the invading weathermen fanned out across the stage in a semi-circle of ludicrous karate poses which they held throughout, as if to protect the stage. The whole place was seething, of course, during this — further shouts rang out, cries of being "co-opted" and other such rhetorical nonsense, while several Weathermen speakers went on at the microphone berating the assembly for their soft lifestyle, lack of commitment, naivete, and general bourgeois values. After fifteen minutes or so of this theatre they left the stage, forming a no-nonsense, grim-faced single-file and marched out in military fashion through the crowd as they had come. They were pelted with various available objects as they left. Ida and I left soon after that. We walked up the street past the library mall and the Red Gym, its turrets outlined in the moonlight.

"What a bunch of jerks," Ida said indignantly.

I didn't say anything, just smiled to myself.

"What happens to them?" she asked.

"What? In the future? Most of them turn into corporate lawyers," I told her.

"I knew it," she said. She turned to me and laughed.

I had to smile to myself. I wondered what, exactly, all the members of this little troupe would be doing in thirty years. I would have given twenty bucks to know — just to see a computer printout with their names and current occupations. Ida and I walked along up the cement sidewalk. A nearly full moon was hovering in the summer night sky, lighting the ground at our feet with a pale glow.

We walked on a few more blocks, up Langdon Street. We passed a middle-aged couple coming down the sidewalk and Ida was silent after that, preoccupied — it apparently started her thinking about what I had said the day before about growing older. I sensed that I probably had her fully depressed on that count by now. I reached over and squeezed her shoulder as we walked. "Cheer up," I said. "It's not that bad, okay?."

"You made it sound so… terrible," she said.

"Did I? I didn't realize. I'm sorry… It's not terrible. There are good parts to it."

She smiled and looked down as we walked.

"Look," she said, pointing, "You can see the moonlight on the sidewalk."

"Yes," I said. "It's very bright."

We walked along up the street.

"Do I seem young to you?" she asked suddenly.

"A little."

"Hmm," she said.

I smiled at her.

"In this future of yours," she said finally, "Do you ever see people from now — from the Sixties, I mean?"

"Oh, yeah, sure," I said. "You see them — you run into them from time to time. Sure, they still walk around, they recognize each other dimly — it's kind of like someone you saw at a party you once attended — a huge party, a wonderful party, it's true, but one that happened a long time ago. There is some tell-tale sign still remaining — a beard, a man with a pony-tail, a bandanna, a shared memory. They were people you once knew and were very close to, but it was in another age, almost another lifetime."

"It's like that, huh?"

"Yeah."

Ida and I took the bus and went home. On the ride back we passed the ROTC building. There was a kiosk out front which was plastered with posters of Lyndon Johnson in a repeating pattern, each with a mustache drawn in, and the outline of a Molotov cocktail pasted over the forehead — a kiosk now fading behind us in the summer moonlight.

15

About a week went by after that. It was the middle of June, Art was back in the hospital again and I was starting to get worried. He was a lot sicker this time and this latest relapse was making me wonder again what had really happened during that fight he was in. Everything seemed to have gone downhill for him since that day. I decided to give the detective, Narmer, a call again.

The phone rang a couple of times, was answered by his secretary, and then he picked up the phone.

"Narmer," I said. "It's Nick. I've got another guy I want you to look for."

I heard Narmer chuckle. "The way you keep losing people, Nick," he said.

"No, this is a guy I've never met. Also, I've got something else I want to talk to you about."

"Okay," he said. "Come on in and give me the details. I'll be here all day."

I didn't make it downtown until about 5 p.m. and I caught Narmer just as he was knocking off for the day. He was coming out of the elevator on his way to get a drink. "It's been a long day," he explained.

"Mind if I join you?" I said.

"Not a bit," he said. "In fact, you promised me a few drinks — and an explanation about that money."

"Yeah, I did," I said.

Ten minutes later we were sitting behind a couple of martinis at the cocktail lounge on the top floor of the Inn On The Park hotel, just up the street from Narmer's office.

"Ahhh," Narmer said, after a first sip, "Ahhh... I've been waiting for this all day." He closed his eyes, obviously in a blissful state.

I smiled. Half an hour — and several martinis — later it was like we'd known each other for years.

"How old are you, Narmer?" I said.

"Forty-eight," he said. He leaned his head back, as if looking at the ceiling. He took a deep breath. "Forty-eight," he repeated. "Forty-eight."

I looked at him. His blond hair was thinning a little, but carefully arranged over his head; he was wearing a gray plaid suit that looked like it had a few miles on it.

"You're married, right?" I said.

"Yeah."

"You've got one kid."

He looked at me. "I don't remember ever mentioning it."

I smiled and took a sip of my drink.

Finally he said: "You?"

"I'm separated," I said. "One kid."

Narmer took another sip of his martini.

"You know," he said, philosophically, "I once promised myself that by age 40 I'd be driving around this town in a Cadillac. That's how I'd know if I was a success, you see — I'd have myself a big Cadillac." He smiled to himself again and nodded. "And you know something, Nick? I made it. I've got my Cadillac. It's parked out front." At this he lifted up his drink to clink glasses with me. "Yeah, I've finally got that Cadillac."

I looked at him. We were getting to be friends — entering that stage that occurs in drinking where you wonder how you ever got along without each other.

"So, who's this new guy you want me to track down?" he asked finally.

"The guy who beat up my buddy," I told him.

"Oh, yeah?" he said, with a raised eyebrow.

I nodded.

"So you want to retaliate, is that it?" he said.

"No, I just want to find him," I said. "Have a little talk with him."

"That's what your friend said."

He looked at me, then turned away. I could see the drinks were starting to take their toll on him.

He set his drink down on the bar.

"Well, what are we waiting for?" he said suddenly.

"You mean, go look for him right now?"

"Well, sure. No time like the present." He stood up and went over and picked his top-coat off the coat rack. "Let's go."

"Just like that?"

"Hey, I'm the detective, remember? I'm in charge of the investigation."

Narmer's car was parked about a block away — the Cadillac I had been hearing so much about — and, as we both approached it we broke up in laughter. It was a Cadillac all right, but it was at least 10 years old and rusted out along the sides. One of the big tail fins was bent sideways and almost broken off. This seemed to Narmer the greatest joke in the world — a joke on himself, a joke on me, a joke on the whole world perhaps. We got in. Narmer handed me the keys. I drove.

"This is it, huh?" I said. "Pretty nice."

Narmer started laughing all over again. He thought it

was pretty funny.

"It's just a shadow of a dream, Nick. Sometimes your dreams don't come true all the way — they only make it part way. And then this is the result." He waved his hands to indicate it. "This is... the shadow of a dream."

"Well, I still like it," I said.

"I've got another car at home," Narmer explained, "I've got two cars."

"And your wife won't let you drive the good car."

Narmer laughed again and pointed at me.

The car was huge inside. It was like sitting in someone's living room. The only thing missing was a TV. When I looked over at Narmer he seemed like he was about thirty feet away on the passenger side.

"It's a great life, isn't it?" he said. He had his arm up on the window and was looking out as we went around the capitol square. We passed by the Wolf Kubly and Hirsig building and Manchester's, looking deserted, and finally a group of hippies standing in a group in front of the Strand theatre.

"These kids today," Narmer said. "Sometimes I could kick their butts."

"Hey, give 'em a break, Narmer," I said. "It's a free country, remember? If you want to act like an asshole, you get to do it — it's in the Constitution."

"Yeah..." Narmer said. "I know it is, but..." He trailed off.

He pointed.

"Okay. Here it is. Pull over..."

For the next four or five hours Narmer and I made the rounds of various Madison night-spots, ostensibly in the search for the guy who beat up Art. The investigation didn't seem to be proceeding too well — Narmer was getting pretty loaded — or *under the weather* as he put it. The tour of Madison's nightlife scene was otherwise fascinating — Narmer seemed to know a lot of people and they all seemed to know him. We were in Paco's, near the square, and we were in Paul's. After that we were at the Plaza and the Edgewater. There was a pool cue fight in progress at Chesty's when we were in there — I had to duck once to avoid imminent decapitation — and there was an almost equally raucous crowd in the Three Bells bar when we went there. At most of the places we went, Narmer and I were a little out of place. The nightclub scene was making the transition to Sixties atmospherics and the decor was changing to match. Also, the people and the clothing were extraordinary: there were women wearing bouffant hairdo's and mini-skirts above the knee, some with white go-go boots, and most with the dark eye-shadow and straight black hair parted in the middle, and headbands and beads. It was amazing to behold, of course — all these people once again assembled before my eyes. These were the years of "Swinging London" — of Carnaby Street and flowery Edwardian shirts and exaggerated bell-bottoms, and it seemed quite odd to see it now, but of course to the other people who were there it was quite natural. The only odd ones were Narmer and I.

I had completely forgotten this whole world — the depth and the extent of it. Some of the nightclubs were bathed in psychedelic lights — strobe lights blinking in the darkness, and others had bizarre images projected on the walls which resembled giant amoebas, expanding and contracting to the beat of the music; in one bar, a montage of slides was projected on the wall of people caught in freeze-frames, and various distorted scenes, and faces, and gaudy images of bizarre colors. The whole atmosphere, at several of the places we went, was lavishly layered over with sonorous, reverberating, psychedelic music. Narmer and I sat at the bar in one club on two naugahyde bar stools and looked around. It was a toss-up which one of us was more out of place. He was certainly as astounded by all this as I was. *Purple Haze* by Jimmi Hendrix was playing, blasting out of hidden speakers along the walls. We sat in near darkness under pulsating frames of the blinking strobe lights and I saw Narmer look down at his hand curiously and move it up and down, the image broken up into pieces by the flashing lights.

"Goddamn hippies," he said, looking at it.

Another thing I had forgotten was that in this year, 1969, there were still some people for whom the 1950's was very much alive. There were a few people still around who were hanging on to the beatnik dream — people dressed like Maynard G. Krebs on the *Dobie Gillis* show, wearing gray sweatshirts and goatees — those who believed the "beat" lifestyle still had a chance, who still went to coffee-houses and folksinger concerts. To these descendants of Kerouac and Ginsburg the hippie experience was simply new, updated, trendy and very unwelcome. They could see their own belief systems fading in the public eye, going out of fashion.

I mention this because on our rounds, Narmer and I stumbled into one 'underground' bar by accident — a bar which featured three folksingers sitting on wooden stools playing acoustic guitars and attempting to harmonize like Peter, Paul and Mary. Dim lighting suffused the place and there were brick walls and a small cabaret stage and an entranced circle of customers sitting at their feet clapping along and swaying from side to side dreamily. This was a bar we had gone into by mistake, as I say, and we weren't there very long. "Jesus, let's get out of here," Narmer said when he recognized the error, "It's the goddamn Peace Corps crowd." We made for the exit.

We went up the stairs in the back and emerged into an alley on Johnson Street. We walked on a couple of blocks, in the direction of Narmer's car, which we had left near State street. On the opposite side of the street I could see groups of freshmen dragging their white laundry bags, tied with drawstrings, across to Sellery Hall to use the coin machines in the basement — something I had done myself years before as a freshman. The two of us proceeded on down the sidewalk. It was a warm, clear summer night.

We stopped off in another bar, finally — Nick's, on State Street. The long walk from Johnson Street seemed to have sobered Narmer off somewhat, but he was still — by any of the usual definitions — loaded.

"We're looking for this guy," he said, turning to me, squinting, talking in a low voice out of the side of his mouth, "We don't appear to be, but we are. It's clandestine..."

"Sure," I said.

"It's an undercover operation," he said. "That's why it's so secret." Then he asked: "Hey, this guy we're looking for, what is he... a big guy, or what?"

I was getting kind of fond of Narmer. He was quiet, but he grew on you.

"You know, maybe we ought to give up and try again tomorrow, Roy," I suggested diplomatically. Roy was his first name.

"Well, heck no," Narmer said. He pounded his fist lightly on the bar-top at Nick's to reinforce his claim. "We're going to find the sonabitch tonight."

"Okay, if you say so."

We had one more drink at Nick's and, finally, after thinking it over, I decided to bring it up. It was probably the wrong time, but I couldn't help it. It had to happen sometime. And sometimes when you're both drinking is the best time. I took a deep breath. "You know, Narmer, I've got a problem," I said to him. "Mind if I run it by you?"

"Sure," he said.

"Well, you're going to find it a little hard to believe."

"I've heard a lot of weird stuff," he said. "Try me."

"You haven't heard anything as weird as this," I told him.

"Try me," he said again.

"You'll give it a chance? You'll keep an open mind?"

He nodded, shifted around a little, preparing to listen.

"I'm all set," he said. "All ears. Fire away."

"Okay," I said. "Here it goes—" I looked around again,

still not sure of how to proceed. Finally I said: "I know your daughter."

His eyes opened a little at this.

"My daughter is nine years old," he said.

"Yeah, I know. Her name is Lakey."

I took another deep breath and looked around Nick's bar. It didn't look a whole lot different than it would twenty-five years later, in the 1990's. A handful of people were gathered at the far end of the bar, near the window, sitting behind mixed drinks.

Finally I said: "Let me tell you a story, Narmer. It's a story about the future, okay? It's twenty-five years from now. It's a story about a guy who is dying, this father, see — he's had a heart attack, and he's on his deathbed, and his daughter, who is about, let's say, thirty-five years old or so is coming to visit him. That's the story." I paused and looked around the bar again. I wasn't doing much better than Narmer. I'd had a little too much to drink myself. Narmer looked at me, in a deadpan way. I went on: "Anyway, the father is dying, mostly from alcoholism and a few other related diseases, because he should have quit drinking a little earlier in life, but the years went by, as they do, and then it was too late — it's the mid-1990's, you see, in this story, and he's in this hospital hooked up to all these machines, and his daughter comes to visit him and she's pretty sad about it. They were always pretty close, you see, the father and the daughter, so it's really upsetting to her — she's feeling pretty distraught — in fact, if truth be known, it's really ruining her life. A little after that in the story the father dies, and life goes on pretty much like before and the daughter gets over it and goes back to her life. But she doesn't really get over it, and a few months later, on a night when she's feeling particularly low and has had a little too much to drink, she takes her own life."

I stopped, took another sip of my drink, and looked around. Lakey didn't kill herself, but I tacked that on to the story for emphasis — just to get his attention.

Narmer just looked at me. He didn't say anything. In

his line of work he'd heard it all, all right, but he'd never heard that one.

He kept looking. I didn't say anything either.

He lit a cigarette, waved out the match. "That's it?" he said finally, "End of story?"

I shrugged. "Yeah. That's it. End of story."

Narmer kept looking at me, over the edge of his glass. Neither one of us said anything. The jukebox started playing a song by Arlo Guthrie.

"What?" Narmer said finally.

"You got to back off on the drinking, Narmer," I said.

"What, I'm the father in the story?"

I looked around the bar, casually, noncommittal.

Narmer took a drag on his cigarette, blew a cloud of smoke upwards, then looked at me again.

"You might have to douse the cigarettes too," I said. "I think that was part of the problem."

Narmer tapped the cigarette slowly and thoughtfully over a bar ashtray — one of the square kind, made of glass — then looked at me again.

"You know, first of all," he said, "not too many people commit suicide over a death in the family. That's one of the things a detective learns. So the story doesn't ring true."

"Oh I'm sure you're right," I said. "It's not very common. But it happens. And in this case it happened."

Narmer looked at me skeptically, exhaled another cloud of cigarette smoke, and then looked some more. The conversation had sobered him off somewhat, if nothing else, trying to figure it out.

I drew another breath and plunged on:

"It sounds like quite a long ways off, doesn't it — the 1990's? But it really isn't. Actually, it's right around the corner. It comes around pretty quick, and it *does* come around, Narmer — it's not some mythical far-off time that will never get here."

There was another long thoughtful silence, neither one of us saying anything, Narmer smoking quietly and looking at me.

"You never wanted to find this guy, did you?" he said. "You just did it to talk to me."

"No, as a matter of fact," I said. "I did want to find him — and I still do. I need you for that. It just worked out that it gave me the chance to bring this up."

Narmer thought that one over, glancing around.

"And that money you gave me the other day—" he said.

"—Was the real thing," I finished the sentence for him.

"And you got it from some time in the future because that's where you came from," he said. "Is that what you want me to believe?"

I didn't say anything to that.

Narmer shook his head, smiled to himself and stubbed his cigarette out slowly in the nearby ashtray. It was almost a half-smile — of satisfaction. He'd figured it out — he'd solved the puzzle. He said: "You know, I always said to my wife, we gotta get out of this town — there's too many nutty people here." He smiled to himself and shook his head. "What did you do — land in a UFO or something?"

There wasn't much I could say to that, but I still had some of the money I had arrived with. I had some coins in my pocket. It wasn't much, but it was something. A couple of quarters, a few dimes, nickels, and some bright, newly minted pennies. I had almost spent them on several occasions, but at the last moment had quickly grabbed them back. On the bottom right-hand corner of one of the pennies, stamped clear and bold, was the date, "1991." I took it out, turned it over a couple times in my fingers and placed it on the bar with a click. Narmer slid it over, picked it up, turned it over.

"Easy," he said. "You can get these at any amusement park."

"Can you?" I said. "Where? The State Fair?"

"Okay, but they can be made."

I took a few more out of my pocket, half a handful, and spread them out across the bar. "I must have gone to a lot of trouble getting all these made up, Narmer," I said.

He didn't say anything to that.

"You're the detective, Narmer," I said. "You know all about motives. What would be my motive for doing that? Just to razz you in Nick's bar — get a rise out of you?" I asked. "Think about it. Why would I do it? What would be my motive?"

I took a sip of my beer and glanced around.

"Quit drinking, Narmer," I said finally.

"So you're my guardian angel from the future," he said. He glanced up at the ceiling and chuckled to himself. "Jesus, I always knew it would come to this. I *better* quit drinking — I'll be seeing pink elephants next." He looked at me again and laughed a second time. "My guardian angel — I thought you'd be better looking."

"Sorry," I said, smiling back.

He turned over a few of the other coins, then raised his eyes. Our eyes met again and he looked at me.

"Hey, you don't have to believe me," I said. "You don't have to believe any of this. Hell, I wouldn't either. But do me a favor and just knock off the drinking a little, okay? Just back off a little... She's a nice kid..."

He thought about it for awhile. His brow furrowed; he didn't say anything for a long time. Finally he said, almost tenderly:

"Let's suppose for the sake of argument that you're right, and through some freak this was true. What would she be like in this future — my daughter?"

"What would she be like?" I said, surprised by the question. "I don't know... Terrific. Wonderful. She has a lot of enthusiasm, she's well-liked, lot of friends..."

"Yeah? Lot of friends?" He liked that. He was smiling. "She turned out pretty good, huh?"

I smiled back. "Yeah, Narmer, she turned out pretty good. In fact, she turned out *very* good. Until she kills herself."

That brought him back to earth. The smile went away.

"Just knock off the drinking, Narmer," I said softly.

He didn't say anything to that.

"You gonna remember all this in the morning?" I asked

him.

"Sure, but I just don't see it as a problem," he said.

"Well you don't have to see her crying in the mid-Nineties..." I said.

I got in the driver's seat of the massive Cadillac to take him home. On the way to Narmer's house we stopped briefly at Showalter's Strip Joint, the place where Art had gotten beaten up, just to take a look around. There was hardly anyone there, the place was large, dark and vacant. A young woman in a G-string and a bored look was going through the motions on a lighted runway, under a bank of spotlights. A pair of tassels on her breasts were making exotic circles in opposite directions, and she gave us a practiced seductive look out from under a ton of makeup and eye-shadow. It was just us and about four or five others, all men, all seated in the front row. A bartender in a white coat was polishing a glass, watching her too. It had been Narmer's idea to stop in since it was on his way home, to get a glass of "soda pop," as he put it, but he fell asleep almost the moment they set his drink in front of him, and never touched it.

"We'll find him," he said with his eyes closed. "The new sober Narmer will find him." The stripper with the tassels hovered right above us, attracted to the two newcomers, but I don't think Narmer noticed.

"Do you mind?" I said to her, and she turned away.

Narmer was sitting in a kind of slouch already, his head tilting downward from time to time, his eyes opening and closing alternately. It was time to go home, if truth be known.

"I don't see him around," Narmer said.

"You got your eyes closed, Narmer," I reminded him.

"Oh, yeah. That's probably why. Let's go home," he said.

"Okay."

"I know who he is, anyway," he said suddenly, quite

offhand.

"You do?"

"Well, yeah. Sure. It's in the police report."

"What was his name?"

"Hell, I can't remember." Narmer chuckled to himself, then glanced around the bar and yawned heavily.

"Come on, Roy," I said. "I'll take you home."

As we were getting to our feet the house lights came on and the few remaining customers headed for the exits. Narmer lived on the northeast side of town, as it turned out, near the Oscar Mayer meat factory and because of that there was a pungent aroma in the summer air when we drove up to his house. I took him under the arm and helped him up the short sidewalk and in the front door. Inside was furnished modestly: a kitchen table with a yellow oilcloth covering, chairs, an armchair in one corner and a small black and white TV. A row of glass figurines stood ranged on a shelf along the wall. Ten yards of beige carpet stretched into a short hallway. I sat Narmer down in the armchair, where he slumped to the side and dozed, and went in to use the bathroom. Coming back I was jolted: I felt a chill go down my spine. I looked for a long moment at one door in the hallway. I stood frozen, looking at it, and almost had to physically restrain myself from opening it and looking in. It was a hallway bedroom... where a nine-year-old Lakey would be sleeping, probably with her arm around a teddy bear or some other stuffed animal, dreaming the dreams of young girls.

I jostled Narmer awake on my way out and told him I'd bring the car around next day and he waved at me without looking up. I glanced back at the house as I pulled away from the curb. Narmer would have gotten this house cheap, I thought, because of its closeness to the meat factory. Off to the left in the darkness, as I drove, was a huge dark field which I knew would someday be a large, gleaming shopping center. Now it was just a large patch of darkness with a *For Sale* sign in front. It made me think about investments. It made me think about the opportunities for investing in the future if you knew how the future turned out; it made me think of the concept of buying cheap and selling dear. I thought about land always being a good place to put one's money. Then I forgot about it and drove off in the direction of the Capitol Square, the Cadillac's tail-fins glinting in the moonlight.

16

L ate afternoon on a stifling, humid summer day in mid-
July. A Saturday. I was returning from the Capitol
Square and I stopped and watched, briefly, a wedding in progress
at a nearby church. I looked at the late-Sixties, out-of-date
tuxedos, the out-of-fashion wedding dresses and teased-up, bee-
hive hairdos of the bridesmaids in the wedding party. I felt a
minor pang of guilt, as a photographer, that I wasn't off somewhere myself, shooting a wedding. I stood on the sidewalk
opposite and watched the long-suffering wedding photographer setting up his shots — shots which I knew would be faded
and discolored in twenty-five years, shoved away in some
drawer, possibly, gathering dust. I stood on the curbside watching the photographer with his Roliflex box camera and ancient
manual flash, at the way he had the wedding party arranged in
two rows on the front steps of the church, fighting the wind,
like every wedding photographer since the beginning of time. I
watched the way he was bent down attempting to arrange the
train of the bride's dress in a semi-circle on the steps, but it
kept blowing up in the breeze. The photographer looked to be
about fifty or so, his face red from bending over and he looked

generally hot and harried and perspiring, another universal sign of wedding photographers the world over. I empathized with him. A group of relatives were crowded up behind him now taking pictures with their Kodak brownies, the cars of the wedding party were waiting nearby, lined up in the street in front of the church. Slogans were written on the sides of the cars — *Just Married!* and so on, and tin cans were tied on strings behind...

After the photos, I thought, the traditional parade through town, the honking of horns, the arms waving out the window, and of course, the photographer's car trailing along behind, last in the parade — all events which, twenty-five years from now would be long gone in the mists of time and memory.

In short order the wedding party would be on their way to the supper club or the country club, I knew, where there would be noise and celebrating, toasts, firm handshakes and backslaps all around, and this would be followed — I also knew, as a photographer — by the inevitable dance and finally the inevitable silence — a silence of watery bar drinks left on tables and crumpled-up cocktail napkins with the bride and groom's name, cake crumbs and waitresses with vacuum cleaners...

Thinking about the wedding made me think about what Art had said about Time. Photography was like that, too, I thought. Photography was a way of trying to hold time — trying to elongate the moment for the viewer — freeze it forever.

In a certain photographic sense, people were quite temporary. They were like the moving tourists you see in front of a national monument when you take a time-exposure photograph. If the camera shutter was left open long enough, the solid mass of people became a kind of ghostly blur, and if it was left open longer still, the blur began to disappear altogether. All that remained on the negative was the stone fortress of the monument itself — the unmoving pillars of stone, sitting there through time... People were like that: dancing ghostly around the various monuments of their age — a blur, moving, changing, and finally vanishing altogether.

Now other audience members and relatives of the wedding party were filing up to take their pictures, I saw, right at the elbow of the exasperated wedding photographer. That was always annoying. The photographer asserted his authority briefly, waved them back with his hand. The wedding party, arranged on the steps, was getting fidgety, looking around... The men's side was beginning to undo their collars and bow ties and to shout out clever remarks, laughing at their own wit... I knew without being told what the photographer was thinking: "Oh my God, now they're getting undressed..." He was already leaving his camera position and moving over toward them, re-adjusting bow ties...

After a moment I left them and walked up the street, feeling once again the heat of the July day, and it was as I was doing this, on my way down State Street, that I saw her. My thoughts were still on the wedding, so it came as a shock when, all of a sudden there she was... She was just standing there on the sidewalk, waiting for a bus. It was so shocking, so startling that I froze in my tracks, open-mouthed. She was just standing there, waiting quite casually — standing in the shimmering rays of late afternoon that rise up off the pavement of summer. She was by that little bench that was in front of Paul's Bookstore. Of course. Of course. And how could I have forgotten about her? My ex-wife... She would have been around here then, as Ida pointed out, walking these streets, riding the buses... This was a younger version, of course — that was one of the shocking things about it — this was a year or so earlier, in fact, before I had even known her. I stood riveted, frozen to the spot and looked on in fascination. It was just so odd: like a younger version — a sculpture with some of the lines removed, the face smooth, softer, more carefree. I watched with a mixture of awe and curiosity and, for some reason, a little sadness.

Diane. Diane of the Ambiguities — that was what I called her — my nickname for her. Tall and slender with short blond hair. A rather aloof bearing, if you didn't know her — if you just saw her at a distance — a little on the icy side. Something to shut people out if she didn't know them — or at least *until* she knew them. And now, without a moment's warning, here she was in my line of vision — standing in her natty summer outfit in the midst of these wavy heat lines rising up from the sidewalk of July. Just standing there as innocent and casual as you please. I didn't know what to do.

I stopped, unable to move, my eyes fixed on her. I didn't know if I should go backward or forward. I watched as she looked in her handbag, got something out of it, looked at her wristwatch to check the time. Then she put her hand up to her forehead and squinted up the street for the bus. I had a quirky, perverse impulse to go over to her, to introduce myself. Just to walk over, start up a conversation. I thought about it for a moment. And finally, the more I thought about it, I realized I didn't have a choice. I had to. I had to speak to her — meet her. Yes, the more I thought about it, the more I saw there just wasn't any other course of action.

Yet still I hesitated. I am forced to admit here that my intentions were not entirely honorable in this regard. There was a certain mischievous element involved. After all, this was the woman who had put my suitcases on the front doorstep on numerous occasions. This was the woman who was adept at arguing, criticism, accusations, and who, in time, managed to clean me out, financially speaking — or at least my checking account. Okay, I was partly to blame. That was probably true. But this — seeing her so suddenly — it was... just so surprising... She looked beautiful, really — stunning. It wasn't how I remembered her. She looked even more beautiful, somehow, than when I first met her. I walked past Paul's Bookstore quite innocently, nonchalantly, strolling along, gazing in the window. Next to me, the elderly black man named Snowball was washing a window, standing with his old tattered clothes and white beard and mop bucket and he looked me over curiously. I stood for a moment staring at the display in the window of Paul's Bookstore, and there, standing behind his desk sorting through a pile of books, as he always was, was the short figure of Paul himself. One of the wooden bookshelves had been moved outside the shop on the summer day and set up next to the door, and I went over to it and picked up a paperback and began paging through it idly, meanwhile glancing out of the corner of my eye toward the bus stop. Classical music filtered out of the front door of the bookshop. I could feel the adrenalin pumping; I was conscious of my heart beating faster; still I hesitated, not knowing if I could do it... I considered it carefully. Obviously, I had the upper hand here — I had certain conversational advantages: for one thing, I knew Diane's entire past and her future. That made things rather easy, from a conversational standpoint. Almost foolproof. Thinking of it in this way, I grew more confident and took a few quick steps forward, in the direction of the bus stop, took a deep breath, bent slightly to the side, and said:

"Excuse me, your name wouldn't be Diane, would it?"

"Why, yes," she said with surprise.

"Are you from Chicago, by any chance?"

"Why, yes I am," she said again, with more surprise.

She had more of a peaches-and-cream complexion — more so than when I would know her later — more angelic, more innocent-looking. She wore a well-pressed yellow suit, complete with yellow bracelets, and her brown eyes looked softer and more beautiful than I remembered.

"Excuse me," I said. "I have to explain: I'm a friend of Taylor Ellis... do you know him?"

"Why yes, I know him very well..." she said. Taylor Ellis was a mutual friend.

Diane had her head tilted to the side in her familiar way, a way I would see it tilted hundreds, if not millions of times. She pinched the lobe of her ear lightly, to go along with it.

I introduced myself and she extended her hand, politely but guardedly. I shook it.

"Could I... speak with you for a moment?" I said finally, "I realize it's rather unusual, but, do you have five minutes...?"

"I'm sorry," she said. "I'm waiting for a bus."

"Well, it's very important," I said. "In fact, it's... it's about Taylor. I'm afraid he's in trouble. Big trouble. I'd be willing to pay for a cab for you, even, if I could just speak to you for a couple of minutes."

Diane gave me a brief apprehensive look, hearing about Taylor, then gave me her highly skeptical look — one I knew very well — but I could tell from her expression that she was going to go along with it. I knew it about two minutes before she did. She was suspicious though. "Where do you want to go?" she said, looking around, mildly annoyed. I suggested we go to the nearby Union Terrace, and after a faint, audible sigh, she agreed. We walked down the sidewalk past the University Bookstore, past the Kollege Klub tavern and crossed diagonally over the library mall. The ground around the fountain was now summer-green, thick, well-clipped. Diane looked at me suspiciously from time to time out of the corner of her eye as we walked. She carried her handbag in front of her, protectively. I could still feel my heart thumping in my chest.

"Are you a student?" she asked, just to make conversation, "Or a teaching assistant?"

"Yes," I said. "I'm a graduate student..."

"Oh, in what subject?" she asked.

"Ah... photography," I said.

I suddenly felt entitled to draw this out a little, remembering the way Diane threw me out of the house the last time we spoke. I had no misgivings about taking up a few minutes of her time. After all, in my view she had been clearly in the wrong — even if it was for things that wouldn't happen until twenty years from now, in the distant future. It should also be mentioned that she took our 14-year-old daughter along with her when she left, packed everything up and went out the door. If she felt a little uncomfortable now, well... that was too bad. At least, that's the way I was feeling.

I held the heavy entrance doors for her and we went in

through the Memorial Union, passed through the front hall-way, where there were numerous tables set up for signing anti-war petitions, on in through the semi-darkness of the Rathskel-ler, and out again through the back doors to the outside terrace where we took seats at a metal table under the trees. It was still very warm there, almost oppressively so, even in the shade, but there was a nice breeze off the lake which helped a little. A girl in a waitress outfit soon appeared before us and I ordered us each a lemonade.

"Now, what is it that's so important about Taylor?" she inquired, as soon as we had sat down.

"It's a beautiful day, isn't it?" I said.

"Yes," she said, "it is," with a hint of irritation.

"It's the kind of day that reminds a person of... well, sitting in the sidewalk cafes in Paris." I said this rather wist-fully, as if off the top of my head. Diane had been to Paris, I knew, on a student semester once, and had boasted for years that it was the greatest thing that ever happened to her. I saw her eyes light up when I mentioned it, though they quickly dimmed again as she tried to hide it. I definitely had her atten-tion though.

"Oh, have you been to Paris?" she inquired, rather nonchalantly.

"Yes," I said. "I stayed near the St. Germaine district."

That was the area where Diane had stayed on her stu-dent semester. She didn't bite, though. Instead, she looked around, as if she couldn't be more disinterested.

It was indeed a beautiful day on the Terrace. Shadows from trees overhead made dark moving outlines on the stones at our feet. The water of the lake was brilliant blue and tiny triangles of sailboats were bent into the wind in the distance, white specks moving along on the horizon. A line of ducks passed along the pathway by the lake in an orderly fashion. Students walked by the water, their hair blowing in the breeze.

Sitting under the pleasant shade of the trees, in one of the metal cafe chairs, the Union Terrace seemed as if it had shrunk somewhat, in size. It just seemed smaller somehow.

From this I deduced that the Union Terrace I knew — the one of modern day — must have been expanded at some time or another. It was definitely a smaller version of what it would one day become. I was beginning to get used to this form of 'backward deduction' — seeing something which appeared to have shrunk, and realizing that at some point in the future it must have been expanded without my having been aware of it. In such a silent, odd way as this did all change occur, I thought — under the apparently innocent guise of ongoing construction projects — workmen's barriers, idling cement trucks and so on — things we walk past every day without giving a thought to, but which are gradually changing the face of our world around us. In this way did landmarks disappear, and the whole face of the urban terrain change — and also in this way did the past quietly and silently vanish forever.

The other thought I had, sitting there in the shade with Diane, was a rather odd one: how many people I had known through all the years — quite simply the sheer number of them. How many I had sat on this terrace with — and not just Sixties people either, but a host of other people in between — a great long procession of acquaintances year after year, decade after decade — people who came in and out of one's life... people during the 1970's, others during the 1980's, the 1990's...

All of it came back to me now, as if in a long genealogical line. The past was not one thing — as we are accustomed to thinking — not one large all-inclusive category. Instead, it was a long, winding trail with people scattered off to the side in every year — often wonderful people, laughing, witty, sympathetic people — but each of them a little different. And the faces always gradually changing...

Diane bent her head, waiting, and looked at me questioningly.

"You know," I said to her calmly, "I'm also a palm reader."

"Oh, really," she said. Major irritation was setting in now. Her cheeks were getting flushed, as they always did when she got mad. She started packing up her things to go. Very efficient, very businesslike. "You're a kook," she said. "That's what you are." A good part of Diane's conversation in these years came from watching Audrey Hepburn movies.

"Please," I said, and put my hand on her arm to keep her sitting down. She finally relented. I felt her body relax. She sat back, with a sigh. She must have been about 20 years old, I guessed — there was a wonderful softness to her, an innocence that wouldn't be there later. There was also an uncanny resemblance to my daughter — in looks, in mannerisms. Now she brushed a strand of hair off her face as she looked around, then down at the table, then at me. Her cheeks were bright red. She looked so young, I thought. What had happened to that, I wondered. Where did those things go over the years? When did the hardness come in and take their place?

She drew a loud, highly theatrical breath. "Okay, so you're a palm reader," she said, "What does that have to do with our friend Taylor?"

I reached out and took her left hand and turned it palm upward, and said: "I'll show you." She sighed heavily and glanced around the terrace with great exasperation, but she gave in and played along.

I spread out the fingers of her hand and pretended to look at her palm intently, reading her fortune there. I traced an imaginary line with my finger. "Yes, I see a great future for you," I said.

"Oh, really," she said.

"Yes," I said. I squinted even more deeply, pretending to concentrate mightily. "I see your past there, too. This is your past line—" I traced my finger along one line on her palm.

"You're from Chicago," I said, reading the line, "a suburb known as Aurora. You like cats, Peter Sellers' movies and chocolate sodas. You like downhill skiing, but you're not very good at it. You played golf a couple times, but you're not very good at that either. In the winter, you're allergic to wool — it makes your face break out. Your least favorite dog is the Yorkshire Terrier, because you once had a bad experience with one as a child. Your parents' names are Rudy and Arlene and they were married in Pittsburgh after the war. Your father is a

CPA with a large firm in Chicago and he's got a slight drinking problem. Your mother is a little on the naggy side, especially about your clothes and your father's drinking. Your favorite Beatle is Paul."

She looked at me sardonically. No expression was ever more deadpan than the one she gave me.

She had her tongue firmly in cheek now — her eyes growing a level stare, blank as poker chips.

"You can tell all that by reading a person's palm?" she said.

"Well, yeah — it's obvious. The part about Rudy and Arlene getting married in Pittsburgh is this little line right here—"

She drew back her hand.

"I don't know how you found all this stuff out," she said, "but I'm afraid I have to be going. If you follow me I may have to call the police."

This was an idle threat if there ever was one. She wasn't going to call the police. I knew Diane like a book. She wouldn't call the police in a million years. If someone was stabbing her, or killing her, she wouldn't call the police. She was too polite. If someone was going to shoot her, she'd probably offer to hold the bullets while he loaded the gun. That was Diane.

"No, wait," I said. "Please..." She had picked up her things again and gotten up to go. Her face was deeply flushed now. Once again, however, I got her to sit back down.

"I'm only going along with this because it's a nice day," she said. She took another sip of her lemonade and looked out at the lake coolly.

I thought back briefly on my years with Diane. She was polite, it was true, but she could also be really mean, too, if she put her mind to it. One of her mean tricks, when she was in a really bad mood, was the one about Nick, Jr. What she'd do is, she'd set four places at the dinner table for supper — me, her, our daughter and Nick, Jr. What made this annoying was that there was no Nick, Jr.

"You know, if you'd taken that job that time with my

brother-in-law in Roanoke, then we could have made a lot more money and we could have afforded more children," she'd say, "before my biological clock ran out." That was her big deal whenever she got in an argument — her biological clock. What — she was only in her 30's then — what biological clock? There was plenty of time left. I always mentioned this, but to no avail. Anyway, she'd get on this kick about Nick, Jr., as she called him, and she could be really nasty if she put her mind to it. The three of us would sit at the table together eating and occasionally I'd look up and imagine Nick, Jr. sitting there — I'd try to picture his face, what he would have looked like, how tall he would have been, and so on. Would he have Diane's blond hair or my dark hair? Would he be left-handed or right-handed? "Roanoke," Diane would mutter to herself pointedly under her breath each time, giving me the eye. She never lost an opportunity to mention the job with the brother-in-law in Roanoke, at this company that made textiles and rope, of all things. She just couldn't shut up about it. The brother-in-law had dangled a lot of big money in front of her once, casually, in a conversation, and she never got over it. Other times she could be nice, sweet, gentle, I thought — but if I heard one more word about that brother-in-law in Roanoke, I didn't know what I'd do. Well, it was just such a discussion as this that led to the Big Walk-Out on my part — or, more accurately, the Big Throw-Out, which is what it amounted to. I threw her out, then she threw me out. At one time all of our suitcases were sitting on the front porch together. But it was strange, too, at other times she could be the sweetest, greatest person in the world. Just terrific. The thing about Nick, Jr, though, that was pushing it a little. That got real aggravating. "That's where he'd be sitting," Diane would say offhandedly, indicating the direction with her fork. "If we'd had more money, then we could have had more children, and probably it would have been a boy, and we'd have named him Nick, Jr, and he'd be sitting right over there. But no, you had to be an *artist,* had to *express yourself* — had to pursue photography... That cost us Nick, Jr."

"What if it was a girl?" I asked one time.

"What?"

"What if it was a girl," I said. "Then would it have been Nikita?"

"Very funny, Nick."

Our daughter usually kept quiet through all of this, bent her head down, ate, hummed to herself, and generally tuned it all out.

"If we'd of just had more money," I said.

"Yes, and do you know how we'd have gotten more money?" Diane asked, gesturing with her fork.

"Let me guess," I said. "If I'd of taken that job in Roanoke, then we'd have had more money. Am I close?"

She smiled charmingly at this. "That's right," she said.

It was funny — I loved her, even during all this crap, I can't explain it, I loved her. She was endearing about it, in a certain way. She always had a kind of theatrical streak to her. Anyone else couldn't have pulled it off. Anyone else, you would have wanted to kill them. I would glance over at the empty place-setting, sitting forlorn and empty and unoccupied at the corner of the table.

"That's right," she went on, "My biological clock wouldn't have run out and then we could have had more babies."

"Your biological clock," I would say, "Shit, what are you — 80? We can have more kids."

"Can not."

"Can to."

Our daughter would look back and forth between the two of us with disbelief and exasperation.

"You should have taken that job in Roanoke," Diane said again.

Well, maybe she was right. I'd look over sometimes at Nick, Jr's place — at the emptiness of it. There was nothing emptier on earth than that spot at the table. It did cause a certain amount of pain, seeing it. Maybe she was right — maybe that's where he would have been sitting. Maybe I should have given up photography and taken that goddamn job at the rope factory. But was it necessary to set a damn plate at the table for him, though? Finally I got so used to seeing the place-setting there, and the milk glass in front of it, that I could almost picture him. I could almost imagine the way he would have looked. His outline was starting to fill in. He was starting to seem like a real person.

Anyway, now I looked up at the younger Diane — this fresher, more innocent version sitting before me under the trees of the Memorial Union, her hair moving in the summer breeze.

"Ever been to Roanoke?" I asked her innocently. She was taking a sip of her lemonade and almost dropped the glass.

"Why yes, I've got a sister and a brother-in-law who live there," she said suspiciously.

"Oh yeah, what do they do?"

"They work in this large company."

"A company that makes rope by any chance?" I asked innocently.

"Well, gosh, look at the time—" she said suddenly. She held her wrist out in an exaggerated fashion to check her watch. "I see I must be going..."

"Wait," I said. "Please..." She had picked up her things again and gotten up to go.

"What do you want from me?" she said, emphasizing it, turning back.

"I just wanted to talk to you..." I said. "That was all."

Suddenly — it was amazing — I was no longer able to see the Diane of the dispute/quarrel/breakup. She just wasn't there anymore. I can't explain it. I couldn't even make myself see her. Instead, I saw the Diane I had first seen, the very first time — the Diane I had once fallen in love with.

"Look, Diane—" I said, in that tone of familiarity one develops only after years of knowing someone.

"I don't even know you," she said, picking up the tone. She wasn't leaving though.

"Okay, who are you really?" she said.

"Like I said, I'm a friend of Taylor's," I said. "Really."

She looked at me with her highly skeptical look.

"I'm sorry," I said again. "Really. All of this — it wasn't very nice of me... I just wanted to meet you, that's all. It had nothing to do with Taylor at all. I'm just... well, I've seen you around, and I just wanted to meet you..." I gave an innocent shrug.

She took a step back. "How did you know all those things?" she said, warily.

"Simple — Taylor told me." I smiled at her and laughed a little.

She couldn't help herself. She held herself back for a moment, but finally she laughed too. Then she said:

"Well, anyway, thanks for the lemonade. I'm sorry I was rude, but... well, I have to go."

"Listen," I said. "Can I call you sometime?"

"You're kind of odd," she said. She was intrigued though, I could tell.

"Not really," I said. "I'm actually very normal."

"Okay," she said. She had a twinkle in her eye now. "I'll ask Taylor about you. If you check out..." She left it hanging and smiled.

"Say — I still want to buy you that cab," I said to her, "I wasn't kidding about that — it's the least I can do, after all the trouble I—"

"No — that's perfectly all right," she said. "There's another bus coming along."

"Wait — at least I'll walk you back, then," I said.

"Well, you are persistent," she said.

I walked her back to the bus stop in front of Paul's Bookstore. Then I said goodbye and left her there. When I got a hundred feet away or so up the street I turned back and looked and she was standing there just as she was when I first encountered her. She was getting the bus schedule out of her purse. I watched her, fascinated, just standing there by herself on the street corner. It was causing some emotion in me I couldn't identify. She looked so alone, somehow. That's what I finally decided it was. I had a feeling of... wanting to protect her or something. I wanted to walk back over to her and put my arm around her. There was something incredibly, awesomely sad about it — like seeing a widow after the husband has died — that sort of thing. There was a tragic singleness or solitariness about it. And watching her in the distance, I suddenly felt tears in my eyes. Maybe because I knew all the promises we'd make through the years, all the conversations and talks and embraces — the birth of our child, and all the rest. It was like seeing someone you'd known all your life and seeing the way they'd be if they'd never met you. If life had been different and they had never known you. If they were just another stranger on the street. And because they had never met you, they didn't need you, either. They were perfectly all right without you — their life was quite complete. There was a great sadness about it somehow. And all the problems we'd had — the whole thing with Nick, Jr. — suddenly became unimportant, faded... They became just a part of the general lunacy of another age, another time — an age I had briefly escaped from...

I kept watching. She looked so alone standing there. Sweet and innocent and alone. And young.

My wife... I said to myself, my wife... I wanted to rush up to her, embrace her, tell her we didn't have to break up, didn't have get divorced... but I caught myself, and realized how that would have sounded. She just looked so young. She was just a kid. That's all she was, really. I suddenly felt my eyes well up with tears for all the stuff that gets lost over time.

17

I haven't talked much about Julie. But I was reminded of her by seeing Diane. Julie was Diane's roommate, who I actually knew before I knew Diane. You could say I met Julie first, and then ended up marrying Diane. Julie was more like Ida, only a little wilder, if that were possible. I had an affair with Julie that lasted about a week. Everything with Julie lasted about a week; she was burning like a rocket the whole time. All through the Sixties she acted like this, just nuts, though she calmed down later. Anyone who went through the era will know what I'm talking about here. There were people like this of both sexes — meteors, falling stars... They couldn't do everything fast enough.

Anyway, I remember one particular time. This was a party we were holding at the rooming house where we all lived. It was one of those classic nights people still talked about years, even decades, later. Scooter Malevy had gotten hold of some "One-Hit Dope" as he called it, and for a change, it really was. It was amazing, unbelievable. People were reduced to a primitive state — they were on their hands and knees — even the veterans, the seasoned Big Tokers, who were used to ingesting anything. Several people were crawling around on all fours in the carpeted hallways, trying to find their way, completely incapacitated... No one had ever experienced anything like it before and several of the people who lived in the rooming house had experienced a *lot* by this time.

Anyway, I took Julie to this party as my date, my chief memory being of Julie twisting like a disembodied wraith, dancing with her arms above her head, moving back and forth in time to the music, dreamily, erotically, her eyes closed... From the stereo somewhere came the sounds of The Doors, in a driving beat, followed by the equally haunting, hypnotic and undulating rhythms of Santana... Julie was moving like a gypsy to it, dancing as if she'd invented it...

A number of people, as I say, were crawling about on their hands and knees, absolutely annihilated. Looking lost... as if they were spelunking, searching for a way out of the cave, or as if looking for something in the carpet. Others were slumped on couches in a somnambulent condition, arms over their eyes, or with eyes simply closed in deep comas. A small knot of people was bent toward each other in one corner of the room, sharing a pipe. Incense floated in great clouds around the room.

The music pounded on out a pair of speakers on the wall. The room had a surreal look — flashing lights carved up the room into tiny pieces... all the people on the couches became ghostly outlines, scenes from a silent movie, flickering on and off at a high rate of speed. Who was present on that particular occasion? Were your friends there? People you knew? Did anyone even know who was there? After a certain point *you* were just there and that was about all you knew for sure. It became sort of a moot point which of your friends was in the room. Certainly people that you knew were there. Must have been. But you couldn't be any more specific than that. Julie was definitely there. There was no doubt about that.

All of these people were on the same page — I remembered thinking that. Yes. They were all precisely and exactly on the same page of the same script at the same moment in time... Probably never had a single group of people been so exactly in synch as this group, for good or ill, whatever else you might say about them... Their minds were in psychronicity, as the expression went — an almost interchangeable state. It *was* like one mind, in a sense... like a single lake with waters flowing in and out of it from different sources. There was no individual separation of mind.

Julie, meanwhile, was shimmering like a nightclub dancer in the center of all this — and had been from almost the minute we arrived — moving by herself, dancing alone. That's the way I remembered her: her body moving like a sinuous snake charmed out of a basket — the world's most erotic belly dancer. She danced on like this for what seemed like an eternity, her eyes closed, turned upward, nobody else paying the least attention of course, except me, who was transfixed, captivated...

She came over to me finally, looked me in the eye very directly, breathing hard.

"Take my clothes off," she said.

"Take your clothes off?" I repeated.

"Yes."

"Right here," I said.

"Yes."

"I think maybe we should go somewhere..."

"All right," she said.

"How are you feeling, Julie?" I asked her.

"Oh God..." she said. She ignored the question completely: "I want to be made love to — right now."

We left the party and drove over to Julie's apartment — Diane was gone somewhere at the time — and we had one of those love-making sessions that happens once in a lifetime; the kind that takes place all over a room, all over an apartment — the kind that practically re-defines the genre. Julie and I set some kind of new one-night record, a world mark that blasts and obliterates the existing world mark and relegates it to the history books. It seemed — in memory at least — to be an endeavor which went on for hours and hours during which we were totally in synch and completely hungry for each other. This was nothing more, or less, than two people who happened to be equally lustful at the exact moment in time, going after each other with all their energy and meeting somewhere in the middle to satisfy this great hunger. It felt as if it could have gone on for twenty years if we had let it. Exhaustion probably was the only thing that stopped it.

"Wow," Julie said the next morning, waking up wearing nothing but her sleek athletic body on top of the crumpled up bed sheets.

"Yeah, wow," I agreed.

"Would you say the earth moved last night?"

"I'd say the sun is probably revolving around the earth at this point, not the other way around."

A week later, as I say, Julie was out of my life and on to something, or someone, else — that was how fast it happened with her — and after that I only saw her briefly at the times when I went over to visit Diane. I'd bump into her in the hallway, and so on, but even then we'd exchange a glance. She'd give me this look and hold it for a second or two. It was one of those brief looks of recognition, the kind that says: "Hey, I don't really know you anymore, we don't really hang around together... but, God, do you remember that one night we had together?"

Because of this, when I saw Diane off at the bus station now, something in the back of my mind was unconsciously trying to work out some pretext where I had to go over to her apartment, for some reason — just to see Julie. Just to see what she was like. It wasn't going to happen, but, boy, my mind was sure working overtime, throwing together bits and pieces of possible scenarios that would allow it to happen.

"Hi, Diane, sorry to bother you at home here, but I wondered if you had Taylor Ellis's new address?"

"Oh, hi, Nick, good to see you again. Oh, incidentally,

this is my roommate, Julie."

    ME: "Hello there — pleased to meet you."

    JULIE: "He's kind of cute."

    That's what she always said in those days. Said it to everyone. It was generally the prelude to the next phase — the next blast-off of the rocket.

18

There was one aspect of Ida which I have failed to mention so far. Maybe I've hinted at it, or alluded to it. Like Julie, it came in the category of "free spirit," which is another way of saying: she was never exclusively yours. As much as you wanted her to be, as much as you wanted to believe it, a day might come when you'd run into her somewhere and she'd be with somebody else. Some other guy. In fact, this dilemma was one of the reasons that I'd broken up with her in the first place. Any guy will know what I mean by this.

What happened was that I gradually started to remember the down side of Ida. It was all coming back. History — or the elements that made it up — was beginning to repeat itself.

It was frustrating — and annoying. I could feel her drifting away again — losing her as I had before... It was like one of those bad B movies where the characters are reaching out to each other, extending their hands in slow motion, but the fingers are being pulled apart... She was drifting away again, much as she had before. And I didn't seem to be able to stop it. And I feared all the emotions she produced in me would die and be gone forever...

It started with a few arguments, and it came to a head one night in early August.

I could see the red glow of a campfire in the distance. I had left Art's car parked on the gravel roadway and walked up to the light slowly, much as I had on my first night there. I had been drinking at a bar downtown, and I was admittedly a little drunk. I didn't recall drinking that much, but I was definitely feeling it. Anyway, it was a mild, pleasant night in August and Ida was sitting there — she didn't see me coming — with her arm around this guy, draped over his shoulder — kind of a big guy, tall and lanky, with shoulder-length blond hair. Dirk, his name was, as it turned out. She gazed at me dreamily when I came up — I guess that's what infuriated me the most — the vague, dreamy look — like she couldn't quite make me out, or didn't quite know me. As if I was too far away, maybe...

The down side of Ida. I'd forgotten about it. I don't know how I could have but I did. Maybe I'd glossed it over all these years, or put it out of my mind. But I remembered it now. I could feel the anger building inside of me, turning like a long, thin knife in my stomach. Seeing your girlfriend, suddenly, sitting with another guy. And Ida coming on to the guy, too, working at it — using all her smiles and all the rest of it... Here was another set of emotions I hadn't felt in years. Jealousy and anger. I didn't know why I hadn't seen it coming.

I walked up to them and stood in front of them.

"Who's this?" I said in the most patronizing tone I could muster, gesturing toward the guy.

"What do you mean *who's this?*" the guy says, combative-like.

"Who's this?" I repeated, to Ida.

Ida said nothing, however, and continued to gaze up at me in that dim way — for all the world like she recognizes the face but can't quite place the name. Is she stoned, or what? Hell, maybe she *doesn't* recognize me. The romance of Ida was fading quickly, leaking out, deflating. It was starting to come back to me now why I had broken up with her and moved to

Chicago. Who had a strong enough heart for this? Not me. It was too exhausting. It wore you down eventually.

"Nick," she said slowly, shielding her eyes — maybe the night is too dark to see me — brushing her hair back.

You invest yourself in someone, put all your marbles in this one basket, all your hopes and dreams, even your identity, in a sense... you really *do* give it all to them, it wasn't just a figure of speech or the lyrics to a pop song — you handed it over to them, lock, stock and barrel, and then there they were one day with this other individual, gazing up at them with this look of great adoration. Hot anger rose in me.

"Nick, this is Dirk," she says lamely.

This guy named Dirk stands up — the tall, blond, Adonis type, naturally, with the chiseled upper body — the kind of guy, I thought, who would probably walk around in the daytime with a red neckerchief and his shirt off; maybe have his hair tousled a bit. In about one moment I had this guy summed up. He was pretty much everything I detested and despised in a guy. At least this night he was.

Since this was the Sixties, I thought to myself, Dirk was wearing the uniform of the hippie. When it got to be the Seventies, Dirk would be wearing a white disco outfit with a matching gold chain around his neck. If there was one thing about these guys, they were predictable. Always on the cutting edge of whatever the current fad was. They turned up in every age. Later on, if an era dawned in which high-pointed collars were all the rage, along with matching gold-ball earrings hanging from each earlobe, Dirk would be right there in that era too — banging gold-ball earrings with the best of them, you could count on it. It was to the huge detriment of women that they were never able to see through these guys. I was bitter. I was angry. I didn't feel like giving this guy a chance, whatsoever. He was with my girl. He was also a cliché, which, in a certain sense, was worse. And now, since I was also drunk, I started getting a little mouthy.

"Dirk, huh?" I said. "Nice name. You from Norway or something?"

Dirk glanced up at this and grunted, in a kind of angry perplexity, as I knew he would. He said: "Norway?" also as I knew he would. That was the other thing about these guys, I thought, you could anticipate their every move — and bit of dialogue — about three minutes ahead of time.

"Hey, what's the matter with my name?" he said slowly, in a deep, masculine voice.

I put my forefinger to my head.

"I didn't know you were going to say that," I said. "That comes right out of the blue for me, Dirk."

I was definitely drunk.

"Hey, who is this guy, Ida?" Dirk asks, in the deep voice again. He's shielding his eyes too, looking up at me, like he can't quite make me out — maybe it's too dark.

"A friend," Ida answers weakly.

I don't remember too much of what happened next — it was certainly my own fault, whatever it was — probably I got mouthier and mouthier until I pushed Dirk over the line — but the next thing I knew, I was being chased through the nearby fields. He's definitely stronger and faster than I am, but I discover that by darting sideways every so often I can throw him off. I'm lurching around — I'm really too drunk to be trying to run away from anyone... And the whole thing is ridiculous, of course — there's a certain comical aspect to it, the way we're zig-zagging along — and to make matters worse I can't help laughing as I run, though I can tell that Dirk behind me is not seeing it with the same comic overtones.

"It's you..." he said, behind me. That came back to me later, as if he knew me.

Finally, it was like running in one of these dreams — or nightmares — the kind where you are running hard, in sand, and someone is chasing you — someone big, dark, and huge — but you can't go any faster, can't get any traction, can't make your feet go any faster, and the person is gradually catching up, gaining on you... It was exactly like that. And now there was something odd under my feet too, something slippery, where I couldn't get a good grip; my feet kept slipping on it, whatever it was... It was like hay, or sod... At any event, I was losing the race. Dirk was close behind me, running — I could hear his labored breathing — and he said again, "It's you—" and he had something in his hand — a club? I remember falling then, still laughing at the absurdity of it all, and the last thing I remembered after that was Dirk's voice saying something else — one of the usual clichés — "I'm going to kill you..." Something like that. After that it was lights out.

Some time passed. I don't know how much. Time spent in darkness, and sleep. When I came to I was laying in a kind of pile of straw next to one of the out-buildings of the commune next to a tool shed, and I had this massive, massive headache. I touched my hand to my head gingerly but saw no blood. There was a throbbing sensation there, however, as each time the blood came around on its physical circuit. I had no memory of what happened; he must have hit me, that's all I could figure. The last thing I remembered was the running.

I got to my feet with difficulty and staggered out into the darkness. As I rose to my feet the throbbing increased and my head hurt even more. I had no sense of how much time had passed — whether it was five minutes or five hours — but it was still dark at any rate, still night. There was no one around.

In the distance I could see the red flicker of the campfire, so I made for it, stumbling, hoping to find someone there, and as I approached I could see, to my vast irritation, Dirk sitting there again, reclined, casual as you please, next to Ida. In a fraction of a second my rage started up again. They were talking together, all very casual-like, nothing out of the ordinary... They might have been discussing the weather. They were just dark outlines, seen from the field where I was, silhouettes sitting in front of the fire. I could see Dirk gesturing with his hands as if describing something.

I walked toward them, not very gracefully, and now I did feel a trickle of blood come down my head and run into my right eye; I wiped it away with my sleeve. I knew one thing for sure — Dirk had made a big mistake when he hit me. Once again I don't remember much about what happened next, but I must have picked something up — a large branch, or a small log — on my way over there. I was operating almost unconsciously by that point, my body carrying out an act of will, as if by instinct. The whole thing took place, as criminals often say later, as if up on a screen, as if watching a movie, all of it taking place in slow-motion... Whatever I picked up, it must have been half-rotten inside for, as I approached, and saw the surprised outline of Dirk half getting to his feet, I caught him full-square across the head with it, but the piece of wood broke — it broke easily in a kind of soft, rotting way, so I figured, well, it didn't even hurt him... But nonetheless, to my surprise, down he went. There was a slight pause to it, a kind of hesitation, as if he started to get up on one knee, but then bang, down in a heap and out for the count, and... after that, the shrieking began, mostly Ida's I guess. I was still holding the other half of the log in my hand, looking at him in surprise, and then I could see her dark outline bending over him in the light from the fire, and her voice saying, "You've killed him! God, Nick, you've killed him!"

I couldn't think of anything to say to that. I was still dealing with my own pain — my own sore head and accompanying headache. I felt sure I hadn't killed him however. It just didn't seem likely — I remembered the soft thud of the log when I'd hit him. It all seemed very confusing — all very futile now. I just wished to be out of there, away from there, away from Dirk, away from Ida — anywhere else.

"I'm sorry..." was all I could say.

She was still bending over him. She had her head turned to the side with her ear to his face — as if listening — but she had quieted down somewhat.

"He's still breathing," she announced.

"Well, that's great," I said.

I groped in my pocket for the car keys, dangled them in my hand. "Well, goodbye, Ida," I said.

I felt like leaving, yet at the same time I seemed rooted to the ground, unable to move. I just kept standing there, staring at Dirk. Dirk and Ida. Ida and Dirk. Ida bending over Dirk, who was napping away.

That was the other part about Ida, I thought to myself. Another down side to her. Violence. I'd forgotten about that part too. There was something a little too natural about it around her. It just... seemed to happen a lot. There was a certain soap-opera element about it. It was like: Well, yeah, a couple of us girls met the wrong two guys at this bar and we got involved in a big fistfight last night during this double-date, but it was no big deal, really — then the four of us caught a burger and fries later. It was something on that order. It was just too... ordinary. It was like living inside a country-western song. I suppose the whole thing was inevitable if you had a lot of boyfriends, or if you believed in living the physical life... I was suddenly beginning to remember all the various aspects of why I'd broken up with Ida years before. It was all coming back. I'd had it.

I now noticed Dirk making noises and starting to come around. He was groggy, but he was up on one elbow, shaking his head, rubbing it. Ida was holding him down, purposely, her body over him, turning him away from the direction I was standing so he couldn't see me.

"Go, Nick," she whispered, insistently. Very seriously too — worriedly.

"He's crazy, Nick," she said. "I mean it. He'll kill you. Or he'll try to... I know him."

Gee, that's great, Ida, I said to myself — He's crazy — now you hang around with crazy guys. That's wonderful. So he'll try to kill me, huh? Well, okay, let him try, that was my reaction at that point. Go ahead, Dirk. Try to kill me. Take a shot. The way I was feeling, I wasn't too worried.

"Really, Nick," Ida said again, pleading, "Please go. Please."

"You know—" I said finally, "What is it, Ida?" I had to ask — simply to satisfy my curiosity — it was like this great mystery, this great philosophical question I had to know the answer to. "What is it with you? I mean, what do you hang around with guys like this for?" I really needed to know. Right then I think I'd have given a million dollars to know the answer. What made them do it? What did they see in them?

Dirk was starting to move around more now, making the usual grunting sounds. He was in the "What happened?" stage. It occurred to me to pop him one more time — it was very tempting — but I was almost starting to feel sorry for him, what with all the groaning and carrying on he was doing. I started figuring we were about even. Ida was still trying to wave me off, however, more fiercely now.

"If he finds you, he'll kill you, Nick," she spoke slowly, "I mean it. He'll come after you. Don't let him find you, Nick..."

My response to that was to take out a small business card I had in my back pocket — one with a sketch of a photographer on it and my address and phone number. My fear of Dirk had disappeared. I flipped the card out and let it float down on top of him.

"If he wants to find me, this is where I'll be at," I said. "Tell him to drop around anytime."

Then I shook my head sadly and looked back at Ida for what I knew was the last time. "Goodbye, Ida," I said.

"Goodbye, Nick," she said.

19

I went over to the rooming house early in the morning and said goodbye to as many of them as I could find — to Alex and all the rest. Then I stood for a moment or two looking around at the rooms, the walls, the staircase, the old Coke machine... the way a person does when he knows he will never see a place again. I looked around carefully, a little sadly, realizing that I was saying good-bye to my past... to things I would never see again except in memory.

We sped out of town a little later that day, heading south in the direction of Monroe, in Art's Plymouth Satellite. We left early in the morning. I picked up Art in front of University Hospital — he was still wearing a hospital robe — and we made our exit. Art had said that someone was after him, that he'd gotten a "life-threatening" call, as he put it, and so we were heading out — now. That was fine with me, I told him. Within minutes we were on the highway heading south out of Madison. I was driving. Art was sitting half-slumped over on the passenger side with his head propped up, using his coat for a pillow. Once out on the highway, a couple of soft touches on the gas pedal brought us up to about 70 mph. I confessed to a certain feeling of relief getting out of town.

"Did you ever talk to Amy?" I asked him when we were out of the city limits.

He just looked out the window, as if he hadn't heard me. Another moment or two went by in silence.

"Well, at least we both managed to get into a fight," I said, changing the subject.

"Yeah," Art smiled weakly.

The engine noise from the car was loud, throaty and reverberating, and we both had to raise our voices to talk over it.

"This guy you got in a fight with," I said to him, "What does he look like?"

"Tall, blond hair," Art said.

"His name wouldn't be Dirk, would it?"

Art looked over at me.

His face was ashen-colored; he didn't look well at all.

"Why, do you know him?"

"I met a guy who fits the description."

I had no sooner gotten the words out of my mouth than I saw a car appear behind us. It was just a speck at first in the rear view mirror, far behind us, but the speck grew larger. What made this unusual was that we were going about 70 miles an hour. No cars were supposed to be catching up to you when you were going 70. Anybody traveling at a reasonable speed would have been falling behind. I mentioned this to Art and he looked over at me.

"What does it look like?" he said.

I peered into the rear-view mirror.

"Ford Mustang," I said, "about '65 or '64."

Indeed, an emerald-green Mustang was beginning to take shape behind us, starting to fill up the rear-view mirror, gaining ground.

Art glanced over at me. "That's him, all right," he said.

I said nothing.

"Step on it," Art said.

I gave it another ten miles an hour, to about 80, and

held it there. I let a minute or two go by, but there didn't seem to be any change in the distance between us and the other car.

"He's really rolling," I said.

Art swiveled around then, looking out the back window.

"Think he can catch us?" I asked him.

"Are you kidding?" Art smiled, "In a Ford Mustang?"

I pressed down steadily on the gas pedal and the speed jumped to around 90. We were really flying. Scenery was starting to move by with that high-speed blur you get. Farms, fences, signs, telephone poles flew by. The Mustang faded slightly, but it was still holding on.

"This guy is pretty determined," I said over the car noise, "He must have gotten real riled up about something."

Art ignored this. "How's our gas holding out?" he called out.

"Fine. We've got almost a full tank."

I downshifted for safety reasons as we neared the village of New Glarus. The car engine roared to a scream on the downshift, as if in protest, and gave up its speed reluctantly. We still sailed through at about 60 mph, however. Buildings and businesses continued to whizz by. I picked it back up again just outside of town and began to concentrate on my driving; when I glanced back again in the rear-view mirror, the Mustang appeared not to have slowed for the town, but had whizzed right on through; it was gaining on us again, perhaps only a few city blocks behind.

"I wonder how he found out where we live," Art said, in a puzzled tone, "That's the thing I wonder about."

"I gave him my business card," I said.

"Good thinking, Nick," Art said.

"Obviously, it was a tactical mistake," I said.

"Yeah, for this guy it was. He's pretty fanatical."

There was silence for a moment, filled only by the engine noise of the Chrysler Hemi engine.

"I guess I'm guilty too," Art said. "I may have blurted out a few things to him myself."

"Like what?" I inquired.

"Like about us looking for him—"

"Way to go."

"Yeah."

"Is this the same guy who was involved in that AIDS business that you were researching?" I asked.

"Yeah. One and the same."

"Boy, this guy is a regular Mr. Death..."

Art didn't reply.

The car, even with all its power, had slowed a little going up the steep hill past the New Glarus woods. The Mustang seemed to have let off too, for the same reason. It was a long, steep grade. The Mustang seemed content to hang back now, at a respectable distance.

"Punch it," Art said, when we had reached the crest of the hill, "Maybe we can gain some ground. This car will do about 140, you know."

"Suppose we get stopped by the cops," I said.

Art laughed. "What are they going to do," he asked, "take three points off your driver's license?"

"Yeah," I said. "Good point."

A few minutes after that we sailed past the village of Monticello with all the grace of a rocket ship, past the lake near the highway and the park where the Viet Nam War memorial would be built years later, and a few minutes after that we were nearing Monroe. On the long stretch just outside of town I held the accelerator down and the car roared on like a missile, up to about 100 miles an hour plus. Landscape and scenery moved by as if shot from a cannon. Farm implements and animals became a blur. It was like watching a movie at fast-forward speed.

"Go ahead," Art suggested to me, "Open her up — see what she'll do." We were moving along the downhill straight-away just outside of town. The car noise had increased to a deafening roar.

"We don't get killed in a car wreck, do we?" I shouted over to him, "What does your crystal ball say?"

Art laughed. "We don't get killed," he assured me, "Go as fast as you want."

I looked into the rear-view mirror again. We were easily going over 100 miles an hour now, the car shaking like a bucket of bolts, but the Mustang was still behind us, hanging in there, though now it was a little farther back.

"You have to give this guy an 'E' for Effort," I shouted.

Art had shifted around and was sitting up, looking out the back window.

"Yeah," he said. "Definitely." He shifted back again. There was a silence and then he added, enigmatically, as if to himself: "He didn't care..."

I looked over at him.

"What?" I said.

Art shook his head to himself again and said: "He didn't care — that was the thing—"

A few miles passed in silence.

We bumped along.

"Hey, Art," I yelled as we neared the city limits.

"Yeah?"

"Buy some shock absorbers next time, will you?"

He smiled ruefully.

Finally he said: "We've got to find a place to hide."

"Why don't we just stop and confront the guy?" I suggested.

"I don't think that would be such a good idea," Art said. "You don't know this guy."

The bright flash of green still showed in the rear view mirror, relentless, glinting in the summer sun — the car racing down the straight-away now too, a half mile or so behind us.

"Okay, Art," I said finally, "You talked me into it. Let's hide. Where did you have in mind?"

Art smiled.

"I've got the perfect place," he said. "Somewhere he'd never think of looking."

"Oh yeah — where's that?"

"The Fifties," he said.

"The Fifties?"

"Yeah."

It took me a moment to figure out what he meant.

"Aw, Art — I want to go home," I said. "I'm tired of all this dinking around."

Art smiled again. "Come on, it'll be a gas."

"I'm sorry, Art, I have to veto that."

"It'll only be temporary," he argued.

"Yeah, like this was."

He laughed. "Okay, you're the boss."

There was a silence.

I said, loud, over the engine noise: "I had kind of hoped to see a few things around town when we got back — see the folks and the family, you know?"

"Sorry, Nick—" Art shouted, "there isn't time."

We entered town like a Redstone rocket, flew past the Alphorn Lounge and the Ford garage, down the slope of the hill and over the bridge, finally entering the Monroe city limits going about 70 mph.

At last we were back in the town, screeching around familiar corners. The Mustang was gaining on us now, since we had slowed; ignoring city speed limits until it was almost right behind us. We turned a few street corners in a broad slide. Art's house was located on the north side of town, in the area by the hospital, and the Mustang came around the corners right behind us, matching our turns, tires squealing, its suspension swung to the side, as though up on two wheels.

"He can corner better than we can," Art remarked, glancing back.

"Yeah," I said.

We pulled up in front of Art's house with a full slide on some loose gravel, the Mustang a couple hundred yards behind us, just turning the corner. I helped Art out of his side of the car somewhat awkwardly, and we made for the side entrance, moving across the front lawn.

I opened the screen door, and we came down the basement stairs in a rush — me helping Art, holding him by one arm, Art holding onto the railing, leaning on it, sliding down.

"Have we got enough time to do this?" I asked.

"Oh, sure," he said.

I got out from under him then and sat him down next to his machine — still operating quite placidly where we had left it, lights blinking, as if awaiting our return — and Art immediately began reaching up and turning dials and flipping switches. I heard a noise at the top of the stairs then, and there was Dirk, all right, barging right in. "We might have locked the door," I said to Art, but he was busy at his machine and didn't hear me. At the top of the stairs, as if undecided which way we had gone, I could see Dirk's form hesitate for an instant. It didn't take him long to figure it out, though — in a flash he was down the stairs — the long blond hair flying, the tall, muscular form I remembered — and now he was holding a large carving knife in his hand, his fist curled around it. "Art," I was in the process of saying, in the briefest of moments, "You better hurry up with this..." Art was absorbed in his task, however, and only said, breathlessly, "This'll only be... a short time..." He was sitting next to the machine, turning the dials, concentrating on it. "Oh, Art..." I started to say again, seeing Dirk out of the corner of my eye — I raised my hand to block Dirk's arm and called out to Art in a last hurried shout and he began to slowly turn toward me, just as Dirk raised the knife...

And just at that moment Dirk disappeared — vanished in the same puff of smoke that I'd seen when Art's car had first appeared under the tree out front. After that, it was just Art and I, standing alone in his basement.

Art's mother came racing down the stairs then in a flurry of activity, her feet banging on the wooden steps, her skirt and apron billowing.

"What's going on, Art?" she asked, all afluster.

"Nothing, Ma," he said.

I looked up the stairs again and suddenly, as I turned back, something else was happening — something odd. Things in the basement looked distorted, slightly askew — everything crooked and lopsided... The basement looked empty too. Pictures on the wall, furniture, everything was vanishing... There was a large steam of vapor everywhere... I felt confused, disoriented, and slightly dizzy. I looked around — it was still Art's house, yet now there was no furniture anywhere... I turned to Art to ask him about this odd development, but he looked different too. He seemed less substantial, only a pale outline of himself. "Art — what's going on?" I started to say.

He spoke, but in a different voice, almost child-like: "To hold time you must hold it, Nick... Hold on very tight... That's the secret." He gripped my arm very hard, as if to emphasize it, as if he was about to say more, but even then I could feel his grip loosening and his grasp slipping away. Then he turned to his mother and said: "Thanks, Ma. I love you..." She looked at him quizzically, and then he turned to me and winked. He leaned forward and said: "Here's the final secret, Nick..."

"What's the final secret?" I asked him.

"Alston and Reese," he said.

"Alston and Reese?" I said.

Then there was a further cloud of smoke in the corner where Art was standing — the same cloud of vaporous steam I had seen with Dirk only a moment earlier... And then, like a couple of holograms that broke up into individual particles and dissolved, Art and his mother both disappeared. A moment after that, I was alone. I was standing in the basement by myself. It was an empty house after that — bereft of people and furniture, silent.

20

Through an overly hasty misdeed on Art's part — a misdial of the controls — I had lost a year of my life. We hadn't come back to the present. We had come back one year later — or at least I had. Nice going, Art, I said to myself. Time doesn't pass fast enough already, I need to lose a year of my life... I couldn't figure out whether he had done it accidentally, or deliberately. All the furniture was gone. And the machine. And Art and his mother. Something must have happened to them in the intervening year, I guessed. The basement was empty. And clean too, as if someone had recently cleaned it out. If I went upstairs, I knew what I would find.

I also knew what I had to do. The situation with the house had to be maintained as it was, because Art had told me he would be showing up in the future to inquire about it. It was my only chance of seeing him again. It needed to be left as it was, undisturbed. Narmer had been right — I was the one in charge of it. I was the culprit — the mysterious 'presence' behind keeping it the same.

Another year missing from my life had not helped my photography business. The small wooden photography sign in front of my house was askew, one side having fallen off its hinges. Weeds grew around it, and quack grass, and the place looked generally abandoned.

The guy who was shooting weddings for me would have a thriving, prosperous business by now. At the same time he'd probably be really pissed at me.

I did a little research and found out that Art's mother had died the previous September. The house belonged to the son, legally, but nobody could locate him.

I volunteered to keep up the house on the condition that the belongings in Art's room be left as they were, because — I said — I had information that he'd be coming back. The real estate office in charge of it said this was fine with them.

"There was some stuff in the basement," I said to the real estate lady, a young woman with a bright smile and a gold blazer, "Anybody know what happened to that?"

"It was probably thrown away when the house was cleaned out," she said. "We were about to clean it out all the way — his room, too, for re-sale — when you showed up."

One morning in early September I went over to Art's house to check on it, and while I was there, Jim Townsend, an insurance guy, drove up.

He was an older guy of about sixty, white hair, in a well-pressed dark suit.

He got out of a brown mini-van which had one of these magnetic signs on the side that said, *All-State Insurance,* and he was standing alongside it with the door open when I walked up, looking at the sign.

"You have to be real careful with them," he said. "They can chip the paint. You have to keep them clean, don't let any road salt get on the magnets. It's probably better in the long run to have it painted on, but I haven't gotten around to it."

We looked at the *All-State* sign together, pondering it, then we stood looking at Art's house.

I told him the story — or as much of it as I thought he would reasonably believe. I kept it general; I said I had seen Art and that he was okay and that eventually he'd be coming back. Townsend was Art's insurance agent and one of his closest friends. He had handled the insurance business and the proprietorship of the house. I alluded to Art's hi-tech experiments.

"Yeah, Art was always experimenting with stuff," he said. "I knew it would get him in trouble eventually."

We were both silent for a moment. There was an autumnal flavor in the air; the September sky darkened and the wind blew in a crisp, cool way.

"We were about to clean out the house and re-sell it," he said.

"I know."

"When his mother died," he went on, "And we couldn't locate him..." He left the sentence hanging.

I had obtained a copy of the police report, from Madison, of the fight Art was in. It was faxed down by a lieutenant Jeffries. It wasn't quite as Art had described it.

Art had tried to kill the guy, it said — pulled a knife on him — at least according to the eyewitnesses. That had been his real goal in going back, I finally decided — that's what he had intended all along. A very low-tech solution to the problem, after which, I guessed, he would escape back into the future.

I talked to another cop named Riley on the phone about the case — he dug up the file about the fight Art was in and looked at it too.

"I don't think this guy you mentioned — Dirk — had AIDS," he said. "We don't have any record of anything like that. I think he was just a guy who stole Art's girl, if you want my opinion... That night in the bar — when he got into that fight — you know, I think he went there to kill that guy. I think that's what he was doing there."

"Why do you say that?"

"Well, because he had a knife on him. Witnesses said he pulled a knife on the guy. And based on what you're telling me, I just think that's what he intended all along. The whole thing... I just think he was following him with that in mind."

There was silence for a moment on the phone line. Then Riley said: "He also tried it a second time, did you know that? Pulled a knife on him again."

"He did? When?"

The cop gave the date. It was the day before we left — the same day as my own encounter with Dirk at the campfire.

"I think he tried to kill him that time, too," Riley said.

In a way it made sense, I thought. But still... Art didn't seem like the type — although, as the cops would say, they never do. He must have known he'd botch it up... but maybe he felt he had to do it... He just couldn't carry it through.

I related this story to Jim Townsend, mentioning it as if it was just something that happened long ago, in the past.

Townsend fell silent for a moment, looking out over the roofs of the neighboring houses. He seemed to be struggling with something — trying to find the words to say it.

"I think you're right," he said finally, "The guy stole Art's girl and ruined his life — in one single moment in time. Art never dated after that. It was something that happened in his past, but it was a turning point. It might have been a small thing to this other guy, just another fling — but it was a big thing to Art — a defining moment in his life, when he lost her."

Townsend looked over toward the horizon. He said: "This girl Amy — she didn't die of AIDS, Nick. She's still alive. Art used to mention her all the time — said she was living in California."

A breeze was blowing, and it moved the leaves on the tree in Art's front yard. Townsend scratched his chin and looked down at the ground.

I thanked him finally, and he turned to go.

"Hey, Jim," I said finally.

"Yeah?"

He turned back.

"One last question — have you ever heard the phrase, 'Alston and Reese'?"

"Alston and Reese..." he said with a quizzical look.

"Yeah, it's the key to a puzzle," I said.

"What is it — a law firm or something?" He repeated it, looking into the distance: "Alston and Reese..." He reflected for a moment. Finally he said:

"Not unless you mean Walter Alston and Pee Wee Reese — player and manager for the old Brooklyn Dodgers."

I thought about it for a moment, and finally I got it. I was stunned.

Townsend said: "They won the World Series in 1955, I think it was."

I smiled to myself. Suddenly I knew where Art had gone. Art had indeed escaped to safety: to a sunny and comfortable clime, a time when everything was logical, normal and serene. A time when the world made sense — the Fifties.

21

During the next weeks, I set out on my final quest.

I decided to try to find Ida, Diane and Lakey. It just seemed like something I had to do. I didn't know why, exactly, but I knew that seeing each of them would offer a clue. It might even offer a clue to my own future, and its direction. I would go by my instincts — my reaction to them and their reaction to me.

IDA

It took a while finding Ida, but after some searching and a few phone calls, I found out from a friend that she was living in Sauk City, a small town northwest of Madison.

I saw her on a crisp, sunny September day, which was somehow as it should have been.

It turned out to be a small farm outside of town — what is known in the real estate industry as a *farmette*. There were trees and shrubs on both sides and a brace of elm trees behind the farm in the distance. The drive curved toward the house, and an old pickup stood at the edge of the driveway. Wire fences ran the length of the lane on one side and flowers ran across the front of the house, the width of the porch. Sand-wiched between the road and the fence was a long pile of cord wood. There was a scent of lilacs in the air.

She was standing in the gravel lane when I drove up. She was dressed in a long dress, wearing a straw gardening-type sunbonnet, and I wasn't sure it was her at first because she had a pair of eyeglasses on, something that surprised me. From a distance it could have been someone else. As I got closer though, it had to be her. I looked at her carefully. She still had the rosy color to her cheeks, and her manner and her expression were the same as I remembered... There was a vague air of industri-ousness about her, as though she had just been working in a garden, and was now on her way to pull some weeds.

She was turned to the side and there was a split second before she noticed me.

I got out of my car, shut the door and walked over.

"I'm looking for directions to Sauk City," I said in what I hoped was a facetious voice, looking at her.

She paused for a moment, pushed back a strand of hair on her forehead. "You're only a mile or so—" she began help-fully.

She was a little stockier, perhaps, but she was still very beautiful. The years had been good to her. She seemed a little older, but not noticeably. Up close I could see the tiny begin-nings of lines, and crow's feet. But it was still Ida. She still had the flirtatious Ida-smile...

She stopped all of a sudden, then, tilted her head to the side and squinted at me with great curiosity; I could see it dawning on her slowly.

I waited, and it came.

"Nick...?" she said, with amazement, as if looking me from a great distance.

I smiled, but didn't say anything.

"Nick... Is that you?" She glanced around, and blushed slightly. "Why, I don't believe it..."

A five-year-old with a small rake and a cowlick was standing near the house, squinting curiously toward us.

"Nick, God — how *are* you?"

I glanced over toward the child. Ida looked over too.

"This is Zach," she said, in a child-like voice, "Can you say *hi*, Zach?"

"Hi," the child said shyly, and waved.

Ida, earth mother, I thought. I might have guessed it.

A man came around the corner then, wiping his hands on a rag — a lanky guy of about 40 in jeans and a work shirt, long hair with a pony-tail tied behind.

"And this is my husband..." she said. "Harley, this is Nick,"

"Pleased to meet you," Harley said, and extended a hand.

"I used to know Nick from... a long time ago," Ida said. Harley smiled.

"I'll be in the house," he said. He moved off, went in the direction of the porch. Ida followed him with her eyes, then turned back.

"So you're a farmer, huh?" I said to her.

"Yeah—" she laughed, "Who would have thunk it?"

"When did you get this place?"

"About four or five years ago. We moved up from Madison."

"It looks great," I said, looking around.

She nodded. There was an awkward silence.

"Yeah," she said finally. Then she said: "Hey, do you remember that game you used to play — about being from the future?"

"You remember that?" I said.

"Well, yeah, sure I do," she said.

"Well," I said, "it looks like we finally made it, didn't we?"

"Yeah, we made it to the future," she said. She put her arms out, as if indicating everything — the farm, the house, a couple of chickens standing in the gravel driveway. "Here it is..." She laughed.

"Did you ever see that Dirk guy again?" I asked.

"Dirk...?" She paused. Then: *"No..."* she said very earnestly, almost gravely. "You know what? Not after that one night, when you got into that fight with him. I never saw him again him after that. Did you?"

"No."

She bit her lip, as if wondering where he could have gone. Then she glanced again quickly toward the end of the drive.

"Zach — stay out of there," she shouted.

She shook her head with exasperation. "Kids," she said. Then she gestured toward the house.

"Hey, do you want to come inside?" she said. "We've got some iced tea..."

"No, I have to be going. I just stopped in... I... came up to visit a friend of mine, a guy in town here — a photographer."

"Photographer, huh?"

"Yeah," I said and laughed.

She laughed too.

I saw then that I didn't love her. At least not in the way that I once had. I knew it as every man instinctively knows when he sees a former lover and realizes that what they had is not there anymore — that they have turned into two different people. A conversation is just a conversation and no longer has the electricity behind it. Now it's just two people talking, two old acquaintances. I had loved her dearly, but I had loved her the way she was back then, at a certain time and place — a certain wonderful focus of energy in a certain year, in the sunniest moment of her youth — a month and a summer when the world was at her feet, when she walked down the street and people called out to her and all the world had turned toward her in her energy and her beauty. It was a time and set of circumstances that could never come again. It was gone. I loved a memory — I loved a laughing, dancing figure from a time now gone.

DIANE

I drove over to where Diane was staying — an apartment in downtown Monroe, above one of the local businesses on the town square. I met my daughter at the door and hugged her. She was sixteen now and looked almost as Diane had looked in the late 60's.

"Oh, daddy," she said, glad to see me.

"I guess I don't give you enough hugs," I said, giving her a hug.

Diane appeared behind her, over her shoulder. She looked older, more serious. The expression on her face was that she was glad to see me, but trying to hide it. Trying to look disgruntled; standing with her arms loosely crossed. Strictly Diane, all the way. She couldn't hide the half-smile though. She had the worst poker face in the world.

"Where have you been, Nick?" she said.

I ignored the question. My mind went back to seeing her standing on that street corner in her youth, waiting in the sunlight for that bus. I couldn't get the image out of my mind.

"I want to move back in," I said.

My daughter was in high school now; she was in the concert band and played the saxophone and even had a boyfriend. She was another year taller, older, more grown-up. The music stand was still set up in the living room with the sheet music on it, as it always had been, and the saxophone was laying nearby. The school band would sometimes play in band concerts in a nearby park, and you could hear them very faintly on the afternoon air. I remembered that I was always kind of proud knowing she was in the band, making music in the distance. "Do you still practice every day?" I asked. She nodded. She looked beautiful. "And does the cat still sit and listen when you play?" Diane and I smiled at the memory, and about the long years of listening to her practice. It was something we had in common. We had a lot of things in common, actually. Diane wasn't that bad a sort, really.

"How's your brother-in-law?" I asked, testing the waters, "The one in Roanoke?"

"They just built a $250,000 house," Diane said. "Next to a golf course—"

"Well, that's swell," I said. "I'm so happy for them."

Her voice softened as she added: "—And they're getting

a divorce."

My eyebrows lifted.

"Oh, they *are?*" I said.

"Yeah."

"Well, see...?"

She came over to me and embraced me then, and put her head on my shoulder, and I kissed her gently on the cheek.

Diane wasn't that bad a sort, really.

LAKEY

I made a date to meet Lakey at the Old Smokey tavern — a local establishment — where we ordered a couple beers and sat at the bar, catching up on old times. In the time I had been away Lakey had once again become her usual confident, vibrant self.

"I know your father," I said when the beer arrived, "How's he doing?"

"Oh you do?" she said with surprise, "Where did you meet him?"

"Oh, I just ran into him one time in Madison. How's he doing?"

"He's fine. He's as grumpy as ever."

"He's a pretty good guy, you know," I said to her.

She nodded. "Yeah, he's a pretty good guy."

"He's not still practicing, is he?"

"No — it's mostly fishing now."

"Fishing?"

"Yeah, he gave up drinking a few years ago. He's into fishing now. And biking—"

She showed me a picture of him, got it out of her purse with an elaborate production. In the photo, father and daughter stood side by side, squinting into the sun. Narmer's hair had turned snow-white. Otherwise he looked the same. He had a big smile in the photograph and a fishing pole in one hand. There was a lake in the background.

"Biking," I said to her and laughed.

"Yeah," she said, and laughed back. "He's got a helmet

and a biking outfit he wears and everything. You oughta see him. You wouldn't believe it."

"He's a good guy," I said again.

"Yeah," she said. "He's a good guy."

I went over to Art's house one more time after that. There was, just as before, nothing in the house — everything stripped bare — except for in his room. In his room I found sheafs of notes, essays, papers — a lot of it simply laying on the floor. I picked up a couple of them, and sat on the bed and read some excerpts. One of the fragments said:

" (1) Certain things age by real time: teeth, bodies, even the ability to feel or experience things... Real-time vs. People-time is analogous to having a car with a new set of tires on it: in one sense, they are constantly aging, every second of every day; but in another sense, they are aging only within *their own internal system* (in this case, when they are driven). So in one sense they are hardly aging at all...

" (2) For all intents and purposes, from the point of view of a thought, no time ever passes. No time has elapsed. Yet there is a great sadness about this, in a way. None of the future has happened, from the point of view, let us say, of a childhood ball glove, a clothes closet, a toy you once had, an early romance. From *their* points of view (if they were alive, if they could speak) you simply went off somewhere and never came back. They stay the same. They still exist in their own time frame, their own element. And all the rest of it too. All time which has occurred since then... it has all been merely non-life in their world. You aren't your real self anymore. *They* were your real self, your first self... The rest has merely been you wandering the earth, in a sense, dislocated from them.

"If you once held a ball glove in your hand, one you cherished and loved, and you are now holding it again, twenty years later, no time has elapsed in between. It's like these "multiple personality" cases you read about... The individual awakens one day in his original personality, and thinks: Where did the last twenty years go? Where have I been? His thoughts from back then form a perfect seam with his thoughts now, resuming exactly where they left off. The mystery is easily solved of course: the person was in another personality — but to the person himself it seems merely that the time vanished. He seems to have gone from age 20 to age 40 in the single blink of an eye. It is like this for all of us. Since a certain era in our life, or set of responses, was simply a *thought*, once we return to that thought again the time in between really doesn't exist.

" (3) It is now a certain day in history. This day would have arrived in any event — whether you had died, whether you had moved to Nova Scotia, or the South Seas, or the British Isles. Today's date *would* have arrived, independent of any particular activities or life-choice you had made... And in the same sense, a day in the far future will also arrive, whether it is a day 100 years from now, 2,000 or even 50,000 years. Make no mistake — this is not merely hypothetical — this day *will* arrive. And whether the earth is still here at that time, or whether it is even in one piece, makes no difference at all to Time—"

The notes broke off—

As I was leaving his house I looked back and noted that the house was in some disrepair. The hedges needed trimming and a couple of roof shingles had blown off and lay in the yard. Then I peeked in the garage and there in the dim light I saw something else — a large shape half-covered by a tarpaulin. It was the old Plymouth Satellite with the Hemi engine, now sitting up on blocks, looking very old and out-of-date and rusted-out. Time had been cruel to it too, I saw.